KISSING *in* CARS

SARA NEY

This is a work of fiction. Names, characters, places, brands, media, and incidents are either the product of the author's imagination or are used fictitiously. The author acknowledges the trademarked status and trademark owners of various products referenced in this work of fiction, which have been used without permission. The publication/use of these trademarks is not authorized, associated with, or sponsored by the trademark owners.

Copyright © 2017 Sara Ney
Cover Design by Okay Creations
Interior Formatting by Uplifting Designs

All rights reserved. Without limited the rights under copyright reserved above, no part of this publication may be reproduced, stored in or introduced into a retrieval system, or transmitted, in any form, or by any means (electronic, mechanical, photocopying, recording, or otherwise) without written permission of the above copyright owner of this book

Second Edition: April 2017
Library of Congress Cataloging-in-Publication Data
Kissing in Cars
ISBN-13: 978-1544944395
ISBN-10: 154494439X

Thank you, Internet, for providing the inspiration for the dating quotes at the beginning of each chapter. They're all based on *real* conversations, pickup lines, come-ons, and texts between actual people.

For more information about Sara Ney and her books, visit:
https://www.facebook.com/saraneyauthor/

1

Molly

"The best feeling is when you look at him, and he's already staring. On second thought, that can be kind of creepy..." – Jenna, best friend

First off, I want to say how bored I am just sitting here.

There are a million things I could be doing right now—such as homework—but honestly I don't have the motivation. For the sake of argument, we'll call it a run-of-the-mill case of boredom, and for a good, solid twenty minutes, I've done nothing but stare at the large industrial clock on the wall, listening to the faint tick-tick-ticking sound.

You know that saying, *like watching paint dry*?

Yeah. This is worse.

This is like waiting for your second top coat of nail polish to dry. You know, when you can't do anything but just sit there waiting and waving your hands in the air, trying to make wind because you need it dry *now* but don't want to smudge it.

Time just isn't drying it fast enough, but you have stuff to do.

I shift in the stiff wooden chair, slouching down behind the table because my left butt cheek is beginning to fall asleep. Could I be any more uncomfortable? I mean, if they put these crappy chairs in the library explicitly to torture us, it is definitely working. It's 90 degrees outside, and not much better inside even *with* air conditioning because the school is so old, and I'm wearing a short jean skirt today—a huge mistake with this humidity. No doubt my rear is going stick to the seat when I get up.

Ugh. There's nothing worse than a sweating, sticky skirt-butt—or shorts-butt. Have you ever been in a car with leather seats on a hot day, and your rear sticks to the seat? That's what my thighs feel like right now.

It's so gross.

The library is quiet, and because it's Friday, no one else in study hall seems to be focusing either. Ericka Pierce, a freshman sitting at the next table, is texting—which is, *hello*, strictly forbidden—under her geometry book. The tapping from her phone is almost making me insane.

Tap.

Tap tap tap.

Every so often she looks up at me, frowns, and then starts feverishly texting again.

And I'm over here like, *Um, okay…*

I cannot tune the sound out.

In front of me is a hot-pink three-ring binder and a thick AP European History textbook that is open to the chapter on Rome. Why am I taking AP European History my senior year? Dear lord, don't ask me why! I must have slipped into a coma the day we registered for classes, because:

1. I hardly study at all for this class, and
2. I have absolutely no interest at all in European History (sorry, Europe).

I tap my boring yellow #2 pencil, blow the bangs out of my eyes from the side of my mouth, pull out a sheet of loose-leaf paper, and start doodling.

Heart.

Star.

Square box.

My initials, M and W, which stand for Molly Wakefield.

Then I write Molly <3 Boys. Unfortunately, there is no one particular boy I'm doodling about. My best friend, Jenna, says I have the worst luck because I'm too picky. I'm not sure what that is actually supposed to mean, considering my dating pool is basically a group of hormonal high school boys who think it's funny to burp the alphabet. Example: last week in biology, this guy named Brad Bosner actually made a spitball and blew it at the substitute. He's seventeen years old, for crying out loud—who does that!

So obviously, you can see what are my options are.

Not. Good.

I have no doubt Spitball Bosner would take me on a date in a heartbeat, but do I want him to? Hell no. In my opinion, he's a good representation of what I have to work with.

So no. I have nothing to doodle except hearts, boxes, and my own initials.

Here's the thing: I'm *not* at all unfortunate looking. I definitely lucked out in the looks department, and guys actually *do* find me *really* attractive. But, let's be perfectly honest, guys aren't tripping over themselves to take me out. I also seem to have one other problem: the *wrong* guys find me attractive.

I pat down my auburn hair, which my mom says I've been *blessed with*. If you want my opinion, auburn is just a fancy name for "almost red". It's long, glossy, and hangs just past my shoulderblades, and when I'm lucky, it has a natural wave. Today I'm wearing it down, but normally I keep it pulled back in a ponytail because I'm lucky enough to have parents who bought me a Jeep Wrangler (thanks, Mom and Dad) on my sixteenth birthday, and let's face it—it's easier to drive that thing without hair whipping in my face. So yeah, my hair is almost always in a ponytail.

I have clear green eyes, a pert nose, and of course, a smattering of freckles across the bridge of my nose.

Beautiful? No.

Pretty? *Debatable.*

Cute? Yes.

At least, that's my opinion of myself.

Once again, I hear the *tap, tap, tapping* from Ericka's phone. *Seriously?* Ugh. I want to lean over, smack the phone out of her hand, and send it sailing across the library. Normally I don't have such intense thoughts about people, but this chick is pushing all my buttons and doesn't even realize it—which is *super* annoying. Shaking my head in disgust, I lean back and put my hands behind my head, lacing my fingers together for support. My tan—and yeah, *sweaty*—legs are crossed under the table, and as I point my toes to stretch, I can feel my already short skirt hiking up my thighs.

Eventually, I lean down to unbuckle the adorable espadrille wedges on my feet, and as I do, the hair on the back of my neck prickles. I get the distinct feeling that I'm being watched.

How cliché, right?

Slowly I raise my eyes, covertly looking around without sitting up completely (kind of wishing I had a baseball cap on to conceal my own scrutiny) and sure enough, within seconds I've identified the source of my discomfort: there, sitting across the library with his eyes locked on my legs, is wicked Weston McGrath.

I swallow a lump in my throat as he slowly does what has been described in my smutty teen novels as 'raking his gaze' up my seated torso. Even though he is lucky enough himself to be donning a ball cap, which means I can't see much of his face, I *can* see that he is chewing on his lower lip.

It's excruciating.

Infuriating.

And *so* exciting.

What the heck is he looking at me like that for?

Watching him watch me is like…like a train wreck I can't peel my eyes from, and *holy shit,* I would never admit it to anyone, but he's giving me goose bumps—major goose bumps, all over my legs and arms.

Panic: I wonder if he notices.

Here's the thing: I've never *actually* met or talked to Weston, but he has a terrible reputation—and by terrible, I basically just mean he's a real asshole, totally full of himself, has no respect for anyone. He is the quintessential player.

God do I hate that term.

Player.

How dumb.

I mean, seriously, without getting all Urban Dictionary here, what does it even mean? The guy is what, eighteen years old? Let's be real—how many relationships could he have had, and how many people could he have even realistically slept with to be called that? Hey, be my guest and label a college-aged guy a player—at least he has the age to back it up.

So while he's been given the label of player, I'm not sure if I actually believe it's true, skeptic that I am. I myself tend to be the complete opposite, and will be lucky if I get a date to prom this year, let alone to the movies, unless it's with some creep.

Still, that thrill is there as he sits in his seat, checking me out.

Calling him a bad boy is rather predictable, and it also makes me want to gag, but I guess it's a fair assessment. Sure, it's a *tad* harsh calling him an asshole, because in actuality, he's a very popular guy, but Weston gets into more trouble—so I've heard—and dates more girls—again, this is hearsay—than anyone I've ever heard gossiped about, not to mention, apparently he's a hardcore badass.

Here's what I know:

   1. Last year his parents bought him a crotch rock-

et and he raced it down a dead-end road on the weekends. (Well, I don't know this to be a fact *exactly*...)

2. Last month when he turned eighteen, he got a tattoo covering his entire arm—a sleeve, as they call it. I haven't seen it up close (*obviously*), but I've heard about it from plenty of people. How many kids in high school even have regular tattoos, let alone a whole armful of them?

3. Weston once got punched square between the eyes during a hockey game and never fell to the ice. His nose and eyes were black and blue for weeks.

4. He never attends school functions. No basketball games. No dances. He doesn't join clubs. I don't even know if he has a job. Weston McGrath plays hockey and that. Is. *It.*

5. He has never been seen with a date in public, and I use the term *date* very loosely. Puck bunnies (i.e. girls whose sole purpose in life is to sleep with a hockey player) are constantly hanging on him, but I don't think he's ever taken anyone out before. My guess is he's doing a whole lotta screwing and dumping.

I mentioned my best friend Jenna before, and she just happens to be one of those girls who are *fascinated* by Weston. Unfortunately, I am forced to hear all the sordid details about him from her whenever they cross paths. In fact, she never shuts up about it, as if she's his personal factotum.

The ironic part of all this? Jenna has a *boyfriend* (poor Alex Mitchell).

Anyway, if she spots him anywhere, she will drive you

crazy with her yammering on and on about Weston McGrath and how *hot* he is. I think if he ever approached her, she'd toss her cookies on his black leather boots from all the built-up anticipation and adoration.

Pfft, black leather boots.

I glance over at his feet.

Yup, he's got 'em on.

To be honest, he scares me a little. I'm naturally a smiley, sunny person who gravitates toward happy people—like my bestie, for example. She's got such a cheery disposition that it's hard for me to ever have a bad day. Believe me when I say this: I've never seen Weston McGrath smile. *But Molly,* you might be thinking, *you just said you don't hang out with him!* Well, you and I both know you can tell when someone isn't a naturally cheery person, you know?

So, his scowl must be a permanent expression meant to scare the shit out of people—or maybe it's tattooed on like the rest of him. Also, I wonder if he's gotten his teeth bashed out from playing hockey…

Weston's a forward on the team and has been captain since freshman year, which…is really incredible.

Like I said, he's a badass.

He still hasn't looked away, and I feel the heat rising up my neck. Whenever I get nervous, this hideous rash forms on my chest. It's really embarrassing, so I look away and sit up straight, clamping my legs together. The last thing I need is him trying to look up my skirt.

Pervert.

Really, is it hot in here?

Ugh, suddenly I can barely stand it, and knowing that

Weston McGrath is looking at me makes me all the more overheated. Abruptly, I am frantically trying to come up with a list of friends with pools in their backyards that I can immediately go jump in—yes, fully clothed.

Like, I am *that* hot.

I use all my self-control to not fan myself.

Fumbling with my papers, I begin stuffing the doodles back inside my binder and then slam it shut. Glancing up at the rusty old library clock, I see I have less than five minutes of sitting here left. How long has he been watching me? Should I look up? *Oh my god, what if he's still over there staring at me.* I will die a slow death.

Well, okay.

I'll die a less-than-five-minute death, because that's as long as we have to sit here before the bell rings.

I take a chance and raise my eyes.

Yup, there he is, staring at my face with his lips pulled into a smirk, the dark hair under his ball cap curling up slightly over his ears. The sleeves are cut off the bright blue A&F shirt he's wearing, and as he leans back lazily with his arms crossed, it draws attention to his biceps, which look...*insanely* ripped. He's tall at six foot two. I know this because I've seen his stats in the school athletic program—you know, the one they hand out before games.

Tan skin.

Broad shoulders.

His face clearly hasn't been shaved today. A dark shadow along his jaw and upper lip are unmistakable, even from where I'm sitting. Dear lord it is...sexy.

Really, Weston looks more like a man than most men,

and not much like an eighteen-year-old boy.

Nope. Calling him a boy would be wrong, wrong, *wrong* on so many levels...

I wonder what he's thinking right now as I stare blatantly back, taking in the large black tattoo covering his entire right arm. It starts halfway up his forearm and stops at his shoulder. Maybe he's sitting there thinking I'm a goody two-shoes.

His eyes look black from here, and oh *god*, his lips are amazing.

Torture.

2

Weston

"Son, mark my words: staring is the best and quickest way to get yourself kicked out of Victoria's Secret." – Brian McGrath

The bell rings for the last period of the day to end, and I slide my books off the crappy library table. Geez, *buy some new goddamn furniture already*, I can't help thinking. Rolling my shoulders, I take a minute to stretch my upper body. I'm stiff and sore from slouching through the entire fifty-minute study hall, and I'm bruised from last night's game. Some dickhead on the other team checked me into the boards of the rink so hard I was up icing my shoulder most of last night.

And it was only a scrimmage.

Under the brim of my ball cap, I continue watching as Molly Wakefield tries to scoot her ass out of her chair. In that short jean skirt, it's pretty obvious she's trying not to give me a crotch shot.

I watch her anyway, just in case she does—what can I say? I'm always looking on the bright side of things.

Damn, she's got a great pair of legs—ones I've tried not to appreciate the entire period, because I have a shit ton of homework. I cannot afford any distractions, especially not during my senior year, and not with my schedule.

School.

Hockey practice.

Hockey games.

Repeat.

But seriously...her legs are fucking amazing. Long, tan, and toned, Molly must have been overheating during the entire class period, because there's a slight sheen to her skin that resembles an...*afterglow*.

I can't take my eyes off her.

Jesus Christ, what the hell am I talking about? Afterglow?

I sound like a douchebag.

She knows I'm watching her, and yeah, it's completely obvious she's embarrassed. How do I know this, you may be asking yourself? Well, for one, she's avoided all eye contact with me for the entire period, which is fifty minutes, not to mention the way she's hustling out of here like her panties are on fire, which of course makes me think of her in nothing but underwear.

I'm visualizing a low-rise thong.

Here's another thing I keep asking myself: *Why the fuck have I never noticed her before?*

Sure, I know who she *is*. I think everyone does. She's pretty and popular, and her dad is on the school board. I've seen her in passing, but I guess I've never stopped to *really* look at her. Oh, that's right: girls are hanging on me all the time, so I never have the chance.

I trail out of the library behind Molly, taking in her features from her head to her fine ass. Her hair is loose and hanging halfway down her back, swaying gently as she walks. It's this really pretty shade of brown, not red and not brown. I don't know what the hell color it is, but I like it.

A lot.

Unexpectedly, she turns and looks back at me. Our gazes connect, but her stare remains impassive, which surprises me. I feel my eyebrows shoot up into my forehead because I don't often get blank stares from girls. Mostly when they look at me they're trying to appear sexy—licking their lips, batting their eyes, gushing uncontrollably—which drives me fucking nuts. I'm not *entirely* led around by what's in my pants.

I've got news for you, ladies: *Desperation is not an attractive quality.*

Molly disappears into the crowd, and I stop.

Hesitating for the briefest of seconds, I finally turn in the opposite direction and head toward my locker.

Molly

> "Don't flatter yourself, buddy! I wasn't looking at you, I was checking out your *truck*." – Jenna

"A few of us are going to the lake, you wanna come?" asks Jenna. We're standing at my locker, where I'm both collecting my homework and shoving books into the tiny cramped space. I hold back some papers from falling out with my palm and quickly slam it shut.

"Well...I hadn't really planned on it, no. My parents aren't home, so I kind of wanted the house to myself for a few hours. You know how it is...." I shrug and stand there, shifting my weight, wanting to hit the road. I mean, seriously, is there anything better than having your parents out of the house? My mom, who has been a stay-at-home-mom since my brother was born, is home most afternoons. If she isn't home when I walk in the door, she's usually home shortly after.

Tonight, as luck would have it, my parents are attending a fundraiser for a new girls' school that has just been renovated. My dad works in finance but is also on the school board for our district, so they attend these sorts of things every so often.

"Yeah, I get it, Molly, but can't you do your homework at the lake? Just bring a blanket. Run home and grab your suit and meet us there. Cool?" Jenna stares at me with her big blue eyes and pushes out her bottom lip, which I consider her trademark move to manipulate me.

And…it works.

"*Fine*," I relent begrudgingly. "I'll run home and grab my suit."

Ugh, I'm such a pushover.

What I really wanted to do was go home and watch *Pretty Little Liars* on demand while eating Cheetos on the couch. For the record, Cheetos are a big *no-no* at my house ever since the time my idiot older brother got caught wiping his orange fingers on the arms of the La-Z-Boy.

Food hasn't been allowed in the living room since.

I call it "The Incident of 2010 that Ruined it for Everybody".

Now my mom watches us like a hawk.

"Wear that new suit you bought at Macy's last week," she said, waggling her eyebrows at me in a suggestive manner. "*Just* in case! You never knooww…" She sing-songs this last part. "I want to make sure you have a hot date for Fall Formal so you can double with me and Alex again this year."

Classic Jenna, always with a dance on the brain.

Before school even starts each year, she starts shopping for formal dresses—in like, June. I'm every bit of a girly-girl as she is, but come on—*June?*

I am able to make it home, change, and get back on the freeway in less than a half hour. Headed south to Random Lake's public shoreline with the top down on the Jeep, my hair is flying in a million different directions.

I'd decided to scrap the idea of getting homework done on the beach, knowing that realistically no one is going to let me actually study. Instead, they'll chatter nonstop, probably harass me to play sand volleyball (which I *suck* at)—stuff like that. According to Jenna, I am the only senior she's actually seen read a textbook this year and I need to "give it a rest, already, *god…*"

I'm clipping down the highway at a good pace, loving the way the wind makes me feel.

Free.

Alive.

Young.

I've got on my jean skirt, a plain aqua ribbed tank top from American Eagle over my suit, and flip-flops, nothing fancy, and driving with the top down on the Jeep feels amazing. If you've never been in a convertible, it's like standing on the top of a hill on a gorgeous day and letting the wind dance itself around you.

Pushing my sunglasses to the bridge of my nose, I adjust the adapter on my iPod and crank up the radio. I find my favorite tune, "Gone, Gone, Gone" by Phillip Phillips, and start belting out the lyrics to the up-tempo love song.

"*And I would do it for youuuu, for youu oohhh. Baby I'm not moving on, I'll love you long after you're gone…*"

Is that my voice? Gosh, I sound incredible...

I'm tapping the steering wheel with both palms and can see a red pickup truck in my rearview mirror approaching to pass. Whoever it is, he's hell-bent on a mission to get somewhere and is past me within seconds.

The windows on the red truck are tinted, but I see the shadow of a large figure in the passenger seat crane around once it's passed. On the back bumper, there's a sticker that reads *Puck Off*, so I can only presume it's guys from school and that they're on the hockey team.

Confession: I think you and I *both* know that when you pass a Jeep on the road, it's almost impossible to resist checking out the driver. Have you ever passed a Jeep and not looked? In fact, have you ever seen a Jeep coming down the road and gotten all excited, and then when it drives by you, you're all bummed out because the driver was *ewww*? Or taken one look at the driver and thought, *Damn, that dude is ugly! They have no business owning that sweet ride!* and been completely disappointed? I'd even go so far as to say it should be a law that all Jeep drivers be pleasant to look at. I mean it, seriously.

The current laws of attraction state that an attractive girl driving a Jeep is even *more* irresistible to the opposite sex than any other vehicle—especially one with their hair down.

It's a scientific fact, er...something.

It's coded in guy DNA.

Anyway, like I said, best feeling in the world.

I will even admit to an air of a smugness about myself when I'm driving. What can I say? I can't help it.

Soon I'm squeezing into a small parking spot, and I

groan at the sight of myself in the mirror. What a disaster. Grabbing my bag, I hop out the window without actually opening the door, à la Dukes of Hazzard. Before I go any farther, I lean over to give my head and hair a good shake, running my fingers through it to get out any knots. When I flip my hair back up, my eyes immediate connect with Weston McGrath.

Well, well, well, what are the odds?

He's openly staring. Again.

Leaning his shoulder against the passenger side door of the red truck that passed me earlier, it's obvious Weston is waiting for its driver, who's still inside. Knowing he was checking me out on the highway sends an excited shiver up my spine. I can't see his eyes because he's wearing really dark sunglasses, but this time he isn't wearing a ball cap. Messy hair blowing in the breeze, he's changed his shirt (another cutoff T-shirt) and is wearing Hawaiian print board shorts that hang low on his hips. For a brief second, I wonder if he has chest hair.

Ugh, get a grip, Molly! I give myself a mental slap.

He's just so…so… What's the word for it?

Intense.

What is wrong with me today? These thoughts are so unlike me!

I can hardly even focus.

The driver-side door opens, and Rick Stevens—he's a senior too—walks around to the tailgate and opens it up. I actually have Rick in my marketing class. For such an asshole, he's pretty smart. Shocking, right?

Rick follows Weston's gaze and takes off his sunglasses. He gives me one of those head nods—you know the kind, the unspoken *hey.*

"Little Miss Molly Wakefield, lookin' good. Waz zup?"

Oh my god, seriously? What an idiot.

"Hey, guys," is my bashful reply. They can't tell because it's hot out, but I'm blushing down to my toes.

I'm so lame.

Not sticking around for idle chatter, I give them a feeble wave and scurry to the beach as fast as my flip-flops will carry me. My mom once said, "Molly, you can afford to flirt a little. It never hurts if you want to meet someone special, and you never know—you just might have fun doing it." This is all very true, but I utterly refuse to be *one of those girls.* Simpering. Giggling. *Fake.* The one thing I always wonder is: why do guys always fall for that?

I have never once understood it.

Don't get me wrong; I date.

Have dated.

Do the occasional hair toss.

But over the past few months, as I get closer to high school graduation, it's a little harder to want to even bother. I mean, I'll be heading for college at the end of the year, and as for my level of popularity…I'd classify myself as one of those "middle of the road" people—not popular, not *un*popular, friends with everyone and friendly *to* everyone, for the most part. Yes, I play a sport; I'm on a club soccer team called Lake Country Fusion, and I also play for school. I'm not winning any college scholarships, but I consider myself pretty darn good.

I've got fast feet.

A few weeks ago, when school first started, this guy named TJ Walker asked me to the movies. Jenna was all agog—again with wanting to double date—but there weren't any sparks. I didn't even want the poor kid to kiss me goodnight, which he *did* attempt to do while we sat in the driveway under the garage security light. I kept sarcastically thinking, *Really, TJ? You didn't even talk to me tonight*! Not to mention, he only paid for his movie ticket, and I bought my own popcorn.

Such a cheapskate. Hardly the way to win a girl over.

So yeah. Guys are the last thing on my mind.

But ever since this afternoon in the library, Weston has been on my mind—like, all freaking day. Every nanosecond. When, before today…I don't think I'd thought of him at all. He wasn't even a blip on my radar.

It's a funny thing how a few exchanged glances can change…*everything*.

I allow myself to peek back at the parking lot just once to see that Rick and Weston are surrounded by a group of girls, all eager to be the flavor of the week.

Holy crap, they work fast.

"Hey, guess who's here, Jenna? Your boyfriend, Weston McGrath," I taunt as I approach my best friend, who's lying in the sand. She's sporting ear buds, but I know she can hear me because she immediately shoots up to a sitting position. "Whoops! You better fix your top." I laugh, tossing my bag down beside her in the sand.

"Are you serious? Holy crap, do I look okay?" Her boyfriend, Alex (who has seen this behavior from her before), sits up too and looks a bit affronted, shooting her an incredulous look as she adjusts the straps on her bikini.

His mouth drops open. "Babe! I'm sitting right here…"

"I know, babe, but oh my god, he's so cute." She digs through her beach tote and finds what she's looking for: a hair brush. "Seriously though, Molly, do I look okay?" Alex gives up and lies back down on the towel, shaking his head and closing his eyes. Jenna gives him a quick peck on the cheek.

Measly consolation prize from a girlfriend who's ogling nearby man-flesh.

Alex must agree, because he snorts indignantly.

"Sit down. For god's sake, Molly, you're blocking my view," Jenna practically shouts. I laugh again, because seriously, she's cracking me up. Like right now, she's applying lip gloss. One strong breeze and she'll have sand stuck to her lips all afternoon. "Shit, there he is with that jerk-off Rick Salamander."

"It's Rick *Stevens,* actually…" Alex chimes in.

"What are they doing, putting jet skis in the water?" Squinting, she looks toward the water. "Holy shit, they're looking over here. Oh my god, oh my god. Are they watching us? I can't look."

Oh yeah, did I mention Jenna is dramatic?

She should be the star of her own reality show.

No really, just ask her.

I force myself not to look over at the guys. Honestly, I have enough drama with Jenna practically hyperventilating on her beach towel next to me. If I didn't know her so well, I would feel horrible for her boyfriend, but no one is more caring and loyal than my best friend.

Jenna and I met in third grade, the year I moved from

the private Catholic elementary school over to the public school in our small town of River Glen, Illinois. Believe it or not, the two schools are directly across the street from each other, which I guess is small-town living for you.

The teacher seated me behind her on that first day, and of course I was so nervous, not knowing what to expect—it was *public* school, after all! Those first few hours, no other students spoke to me at all, until math class when the teacher played a short video about multiplication. Jenna turned around and said, "Hey, do you like Lemonheads?" and I said, "Yeah." She handed me a few, and we sat there smiling at each other while we sucked on the sour candy in the darkened classroom until our taste buds were raw.

At recess, I plastered myself up against the brick wall near the playground, determined not to stand out. Jenna was having none of it. Blonde and tiny (which she still is), she came marching up to me in her floral dress and grabbed my hand, forcing me to play Statue Maker with a small group of girls. I remember it well—her whipping me around by the arm until I got dizzy, then unexpectedly letting go of my hand so I went sprawling on the ground. For the record, I never in any way resembled a statue. Ugh, I used to get so mad at her.

But *man* did I love that stupid game.

Best friends ever since.

Leisurely unpacking my bag, I spread out my beach blanket, snapping it open on the sandy shore. Off comes my skirt, and of course, my tank top. I pull it over my head and toss it so it lands strategically on top of my bag. Score! (Yes, in case you were wondering, I *am* one of those people who gloat when their wadded-up paper makes it successfully into the garbage can).

I adjust the straps on the bikini top I purchased just last week. It's a triangle bikini in a bright emerald green that really compliments my tan (and my hair) and ties around my neck. Even though I don't have the struggles many of my friends have with their weight, I'm not the most confident person in a two-piece swimsuit, so I hurry to lie down.

"Look at Britney Renken drooling over Weston. Ugh, nauseating." Jenna is mumbling to herself, disgusted. I turn my head and look at her over my sunglasses as she continues ranting. "And what is she wearing? Like a guy wants to see her ass cheeks hanging out."

Um, actually that's exactly what guys want, I stop myself from pointing out, and Alex confirms it by snorting out his nose. However, I keep my mouth shut and raise my head to watch the bubbly blonde grinning broadly at Rick and Weston. She's petite, cute, and running her hand up and down Weston's arm. My stomach does a flip-flop and something happens to my breathing that I can't put a finger on.

What does jealously feel like?

Can you even be jealous over something you don't have? Over a guy you don't even *know*?

Is...*he*...someone I want for myself? He's so far removed from everything I know, which tends to border on, well, boring. For now, I'm just going to lie here and pretend I'm alone on the beach with Jenna. Oh yeah—and Alex.

Er, and everyone else.

Too chicken to make a move, my butt stays glued to my blanket until my mom texts me to get home.

4

Molly

"Sometimes you just have to put yourself out there. And do something with your hair. Also, showing some boob doesn't hurt either." – Maddie, our other friend

*I*t's early Wednesday morning, and I dress for the day with care. I've risen before the sun with a mission: to be just a *little* unforgettable…

Pulling the white eyelet sundress I laid out last night off the hanger, I check it over once more for stains. It's my favorite dress, and I slip it over my head before eagerly walking to the mirror. I gaze at my reflection, all but nodding approval at my own appearance: spaghetti straps and a deep V neckline (just appropriate enough for school) with lace trim that emphasizes my curves nicely. There is a small set of pearl buttons up the front, right under my breasts, and the skirt flares out to the middle of my thighs. It's just stark white enough to set off the tan I've been cultivating on the weekends.

Slipping on a delicate silver chain bracelet and matching silver hoop earrings, I wander into the closet and stare at my shoes. Do I wear a high wedge sandal to elongate my legs or go with something a little edgier?

I'm smiling now as I pull out my well-worn pair of turquoise and brown cowboy boots. When my parents bought me them for me last year for Christmas, I became the envy of all my friends. That's how spectacular they are. They make me want to dance, and paired with this dress, I feel feminine, and kind of like a knockout, actually.

My curling iron has been warming up and is hot enough to start my hair. I take the next forty-five minutes to wrap my long hair around its barrel, creating loose waves. I spritz it with Bumble & Bumble Surf spray, scrunch it so it looks like I've spent the day at the beach, and start applying my makeup.

Normally, I don't take this much time in the morning to get ready. My mom is probably down in the kitchen wondering why I'm up so darn early.

I won't lie.

We all know it's because of that damn Weston McGrath.

Soon enough I'm taking my seat in Marketing first period with one of my favorite teachers, Mrs. Paul. Short, gray, pudgy, and in her early sixties, Mrs. Paul reminds me of my grandma. Also, she doesn't put up with any crap, so it's always a riot when she unleashes her fury on someone in class.

As I'm organizing my homework and removing it from my folder, a large body slides into the seat next to mine that doesn't belong there. It's Rick Stevens, and he's wearing a white hockey T-shirt with the saying *Stitches Get*

Bitches on it.

Classy. *Real* classy.

"Damn, Wakefield, you clean up nice." Rick wears an idiot grin that I want to slap off his face, and he's leaning over the desk, blatantly peering at my chest. Technically, it could be considered a leer. "Nice…necklace."

Only, I'm not wearing a necklace. Gross.

Isn't he a little young to be a lecherous pig?

I don't respond, choosing to ignore him. What guy calls a girl by her last name, anyway? I thought *guys* only did that to *each other*.

"Do you need a *tutor* for the midterm project?" he asks, raising his eyebrows. Gross, did he just use air quotes when he said the word tutor? "I'm really good at giving instruction."

"Er, no, I'm good. Thanks."

"Do you want a *study buddy*?" he asks, once again using his fingers to punctuate his words.

"I'll do the project entirely on my own, thanks."

"So, how's about you and me—"

Fortunately, he is cut off.

"*Mister* Stevens, *pah-lease* stop harassing Miss Wakefield and take your ass*igned* seat," comes the stern voice of Mrs. Paul. She says the word *mister* in such a scandalized tone that it has me snorting in an unladylike way behind my folder. Rick stands up, stretches his arms, puffs his chest out while throwing me what he probably considers a suggestive smile, and walks to his desk at the front of the room.

Gross. He's like an oily used-car salesman. Jenna

would be dying right now if she could see this. Absolutely in hysterics. She loves it when I'm uncomfortable, damn her. Sneaking my phone out of my backpack, I slide it open and text my friend Tasha, who sits three seats to my right.

Me: *Rick is a P-I-G pig!*

Tasha: *He needs to be spayed and neutered*

Me: *Wanna work on project together?*

Tasha: *Totally*

Excellent. Now if Rick decides to bug me about it again, I have a legitimate excuse.

I spend the rest of the class period rolling my eyes as Rick tries to impress me by constantly raising his hand. Each time he does, he glances back with a deliberate expression of self-satisfaction. What he thinks he knows is beyond me. I can't help but find it amusing, and if I had a blog I'd totally write about it. I guess since I haven't had an actual boyfriend since, well, freshman year, I should be somewhat flattered. But…I am not.

Not. At. All.

After forty-five long minutes, the bell finally rings. I'm not one of those students who have all their supplies packed up before the class officially ends, so I'm still sitting at my desk, gathering my things, when most of the students have piled out of the room. Even Rick has fled.

I take my time entering the hallway full of bustling students. It's somewhat of a crush, but as I move down the corridor, greeting friends along the way, a smile spreads across my face.

You know the scenes in the movies where the girl is walking down the hallway, and suddenly everything is in slow motion because the boy she's fantasizing about sees her and turns to watch her from his locker? And sometimes in the movie a slight breeze causes the girl's hair to blow around her face, making her appear incredibly hot? Well, that's exactly what I'm going to *pretend* is happening to me right now.

Every fiber of my being urges me to look away because, okay, I'm panicking a little.

Because seriously, just like the few times before, Weston's dark eyes are watching me so intently my skin is getting hot.

He's got one arm raised up over his head, bracing himself against his open locker door, and my eyes trail down to the waistband of his dark jeans, which hang low on his hips, exposing a slice of his washboard abs. *Don't stare at his abs, don't stare at his abs,* I chant inside my head. Then, *Please don't let my neck get red, please don't let my neck get red.* My eyes quickly roam his body, and I notice he's returning the favor.

His eyes are raking over my body, too. I silently give thanks for my great boobs and long reddish hair, because he obviously appreciates it. *Thank you, Mother, for the wonderful genes.*

I tilt my head and look him directly in the eyes, smiling warmly.

He cocks an eyebrow, obviously taken off guard.

I resist the urge to smirk in satisfaction.

I pass by and can *feel* his gaze trailing after me. When I turn my head to focus on walking, I run smack into a solid chest. Great. *Just freaking great.* Rick Stevens, of all people, probably on his way to Weston's locker, since Rick follows Weston pretty much everywhere like a puppy dog. The books in my arms get jostled loose, falling to the floor. I don't wait for Rick to help me—mostly because he's *such* an ass—and I bend at the knees to pick them up.

Instead of being a gentleman, the swine Rick stands there and begins to feign a moaning sound, gyrating his hips and loudly groaning out, "Oh yeah, baby…give it to me," while my face is level with his crotch.

I have a strong urge to punch him in the balls.

Here's a million-dollar question: how does this nimrod manage to get dates?

Rick has this bad-boy persona that has girls falling all over themselves to get close to him. In my opinion (and trust me on this one), he looks like Kevin's brother Buzz from *Home Alone*—you know, the chubby brother with the buzz haircut? Yeah. When you think Rick Stevens, think Buzz.

If the guy wasn't a hockey player, he could kiss his free ticket to, well…*you know*…goodbye.

At River Glen High School, hockey players far surpass everybody as royalty.

They are treated like teenage gods.

"Oh, come on." Rick laughs. It seems like he's laughing at himself, but he's actually laughing at *me*. I know exactly what he's thinking—that I'm a prude. My face has *got* to be bright red, because I can feel it burning.

I look over at Weston.

He's watching the exchange intently, his mouth in a hard line, but saying nothing.

Interesting.

I shift to get around Rick, but he blocks my path like

the hockey defenseman that he is. "So listen, I was thinking. You. Me. Friday night." He is pointing back and forth in between our bodies.

"Rick, look, I'm really flattered—"

"Of course you are," he interrupts me.

"—but I'm not going out with you Friday. Or, um, ever." I actually whisper this last part because to be honest, I'm a little scared. Rick is an intimidating guy. Tall, maybe five foot eleven. Big and a tad chubby. Buzz haircut with sideburns, and more of a sneer than a smile. Under his right eye is a fading bruise, and there's a cut on the bridge of his nose. I busy myself by rearranging the books restacked in my arms, and nod at him curtly.

End of discussion.

At least I wish it was. He clearly isn't going to take no for an answer.

"Friday doesn't work? What better offer could you possibly have?"

Gee, thanks, asshole.

"I'm not going out with you. Sorry."

"I don't think I heard you correctly. Did—wait, are you turning me *down*?" Rick is practically shouting this last part. His eyebrows are pinching together slightly, confused, and yes, he's angry. I clutch my books tighter and look over at Weston, who has his eyes narrowed at Rick's back. What the hell is *his* problem? Is he pissed that I just rejected his best friend? Whatever the reason for the scowl, I can't look at him. I'm too embarrassed.

Humiliated, even.

Scared too. I can feel the tears prickling behind my

eyes.

"I'm sorry," I repeat, walking away before I start to cry. My heart is beating so fast—*so fast*—for so many reasons:

1. How often do I get asked on a date by a wildly popular guy at school? Um, hardly ever. Okay, more like *never*. The last time I checked, my last date was in the school marching band and he *didn't* play a sport. Still, an asshole is an asshole, and I'm not dating one, no matter how popular he is.

2. I've never actually told someone to their face that I wasn't interested in dating them. It's mostly via text, or Jenna does the rejecting for me. I hope I never have to do it again. It's a horrible feeling.

I've never turned one guy down for a date while the guy who makes my heart beat eratically watches from the sideline. That in itself could give a young girl a stroke.

Screw them both.

Weston

"I know I've never been on a date with her, but any time I see another guy talking to her, I wanna punch him in the face." – Cousin Jack (a shining example of what *not* to do)

I turn toward Rick just as Molly rushes off down the hallway, resisting the impulse to chase after her…even though I know it's the right thing to do. She was clearly upset, and now I feel like a shithead for just standing there and letting Rick act like an asshole. Right now, I feel like it may as well have been *me* demeaning her in public, which is exactly what I think Rick was doing.

I cannot stand being his friend.

The desire to go after her is immediately replaced by the urge to plant a facer on Rick—right here, right now—in the hallway at school. I clench and unclench my right fist, which hangs at my side.

Rick lets out a loud, satisfied sigh and says, "She'll come around eventually. They all do." He clamps his hand down on my stiff, aching shoulder in an effort to be congenial.

"Don't fucking touch me," I growl, shaking out of his grip.

"Dude, what the hell is your problem?" He grabs a Pop-Tart from the box I keep in my locker for emergencies because, well, I'm always hungry. Rick proceeds to rip open the foil wrapper, making a ton of noise, then stuffs it in his mouth. "Man, you really need to get laid." As he chews *my* Pop-Tart, crumbs fall from his mouth. Now I *really* want to pound the piss out of him.

"Couldn't you just leave her alone when she said she didn't want to go out with you? Christ, you're pathetic." I snarl at him as I slam my locker shut with a loud bang that echoes in the corridor, and I walk off, leaving him gaping at me.

5

Molly

"I am not the Jerk Whisperer. If I were, I'd write a book about it and make millions." – Tasha

A few hours later, Jenna and I are lying around my den, snuggling up on the couches, texting our friends, and of course, gossiping. *Pretty Little Liars* is on in the background, as usual.

"So, okay, tell me again how Rick tried sticking his junk in your face," Jenna says, snickering.

"Oh my god. Shut up, Jenna. It was terrible."

"But also kind of funnyyyy…or…*no*…?"

"You're a shitty friend, do you know that?" I shout it out, even as we both burst into hysterics. I can't help it—the girl makes me laugh.

I pick up a pillow and throw it at her.

"You know, I bet he has a small penis," Jenna says as she reaches for the pretzels sitting on the ottoman and pops one in her mouth, chewing thoughtfully. "That's why he had to grind his hips in your face, so you'd know it was there."

"Yeah, probably."

"Well, Lana Dubois said he does, and I guess that's enough proof for me."

"Well, Lana would know. She's seen enough of them." We snicker. Hey, I'm not trying to be rude, but Lana gets around…*if* you know what I mean.

"So, you didn't try to look at all?" Jenna tries again. "Check out the package? I mean, since you were *down* there by it…"

"You're sick, do you know that?"

"You're not sick *enough*!" She tips her head back and talks to the ceiling. "I try and I try with her… She's *such* a disappointment." Jenna shakes her head in mock disgust, and I throw my head back too before bursting out laughing.

"You *try with me*? How! All you think about is sex, and you haven't even had it yet!"

Of course, *this* is the exact moment my mom decides to pop her head into the room, because duh, that's how life works when you're a teenager still living in your parent's house. They always catch the dumb shit you don't want them to hear.

"Ladies." She doesn't say anything else, but instead stands there assessing us from the doorway. She's wearing an apron and has an oven mitt on her hand. I know she heard the shouting, and I know she heard the word *sex* peppered into my last sentence. I can tell she wants to say something, but she puckers her mouth and chews on her lip instead. This is my mom's classic signature move—pursing her lips when she's displeased.

"What's up, Mamma?" Jenna asks, smiling broadly. Ugh, she is such a brat—but a brat that both my parents love. "Are you *baking*, Mrs. W?"

Odd, given that it's almost seven in the evening. My legs are getting hot, so I stick my feet out of the blanket that's covering my lower half.

"Actually, yes. I started baking cupcakes for Shelly's Bunco party tomorrow night. I won't have any time tomorrow because Rex needs to be taken to the vet, among other things." Rex is our seven-year-old Golden Retriever. "If you hear the doorbell, can one of you grab it?" At my questioning gaze, she asks, "Has your dad talked to you yet?"

"About…?"

"He has some students coming over for that focus group, you know, for the changes they're making to the stadium? I don't know if he mentioned it, but the meeting is tonight."

"Yes!" Jenna pumps her fist. "Ba-ring on the hotties!"

Remember how earlier I mentioned my dad is on the school board for our district? Well, our region was fortunate enough to receive a grant with sufficient funds to *completely* overhaul the sports complex, which is crazy outdated, so my dad created a steering committee of actual student athletes to provide insight—which only makes sense, since they're the ones who use the facility.

I'm really proud of my dad. How he finds time to volunteer in the community, work full time, *and* spend time with us, I'll never know, but I do know he is an amazing guy.

A little *too* busy, but amazing.

"Oh Mamma, you know we'll have no problem getting the door when the jocks arrive." This comes from Jenna. My mom stands there and takes a long look at us before shaking her head.

"I don't know about you two sometimes." She laughs. "Have you eaten anything tonight, Jenna? I have leftover pot roast in the fridge."

"Thanks, but I had pizza with Alex. Hey, did Molly happen to mention she had junk in her face at school today?"

"Jenna!" I yell, jumping up from the couch and pouncing on her. She is a giggling, hysterical mess as she tries to shove me off. "You loud mouth!" I feel a leg connect with my stomach and I roll to the floor. "I swear, one of these days I'm going to stuff a sock in your loud mouth."

My mom crosses her arms and rolls her eyes. I can tell she's trying to determine the validity of Jenna's statement.

Apparently she decides we're morons, because she just walks away.

This is how the next half hour of the night goes: Jenna and me hopping off the couches with each chime of the doorbell, kind of like trick-or-treat on Halloween night. Seeing the first few kids dressed up is always exciting and then…*not so much.* Then you spend the rest of your time waiting for the dawdlers so you can get on with your night.

First arrival, Dean Reynolds, a junior on the basketball team. Before we can even get to the door to let him in, Dean has his face pressed to the glass and is peering in.

What. A. Weirdo. Didn't his mother teach him any manners?

I throw open the door unceremoniously.

"What's up, Dean." It's more of a statement, less of a question.

"Not a whole lot, not a whole lot." He looks around, nodding his head, taking in the foyer. "Start a new job this Thursday, so I guess I shouldn't say nothing's up, right? Right?" His voice elbows me in the ribs like, *yuck-yuck, let's share a chuckle*—only I don't chuckle.

Jenna does.

For real, Jenna?

Politely I ask, "Oh yeah, where at?"

"I'll be flipping burgers at Bub's Grill. The pay is shit, but I need a job that's flexible with my practice schedule." He shrugs.

"Yeah, I can imagine," Jenna says. "You guys are having a great year. I'm surprised you even *have* a job."

"My dad said he'd kick my ass if I sat around scratching my balls when I didn't have practice, so it's not like I had much of a choice." Dean's eyes are roaming around the room, and it looks like he's casing the joint. Suddenly his phone beeps, and he immediately pulls it out like his life depends on it, flips it open, and begins texting.

Great. Weird *and* rude. What a pleasant combination.

We're spared from any further conversation by the arrival of Kayla McQueen, volleyball star.

"Hey, guys!" She bounds in through the open door and greets us all enthusiastically. I stare at Dean and Kayla standing next to each other in the entry of my house. Wow, they're tall. I mean, I'm no shorty myself, but they tower over me.

"Wow, you guys are both *so tall*," I blurt out. Crap, why would I say that out loud?

"*Duh.*" This from Jenna. Remind me to thank her later for that.

Now things are just awkward.

"Okay, so…let me just take you down the hall to my dad's office. He's been waiting." I lead them into my father's office, to which he's added an extra table and chairs in a temporary meeting spot. "Dad, first arrivals are here," I announce. My dad gets up from behind his massive desk and walks over with his arm extended, greeting Dean and Kayla with a shake of the hand before turning to me.

"Thanks, sweetheart." My dad puts his arm around me then. "I'm only waiting on the boys from the hockey team, so once they get here you're off the hook." He kisses the top of my head and shoos me on my way.

Wait, what?

The boys from the hockey team? Ugh, of course they're going to be here. They play in the sports complex almost all year long; why didn't this occur to me before?

Before I can let it sink in, the doorbell chimes again.

I race to the powder room in the hallway, flip on the light, and stare into the mirror to assess the day's damage. After getting home from soccer practice, I didn't give much thought to my appearance and tossed on gray Victoria's Secret PINK sweatpants with a purple tank top. My hair is still damp from the shower I took over an hour ago, and of course I have not a drop of makeup on.

Groaning, I make my way down the hall.

My angst skyrockets as my spirits deflate.

When I get to the foyer, it's not who I'm expecting—and hoping—to see, and I think my shoulders sag in disappointment. Yes, they actually sag. The last arrivals are Derek Hanson and Adam Something-or-other, a couple sophomores I don't really know too much about, and not Weston McGrath.

Jenna, however, is neither phased nor disappointed and is flirting up a storm in the entryway.

"Oooh, Molly, come see who's here," she chirps in a flirtatious voice.

I saunter over as casually as I can. "So, guys, you're the chosen ones, huh?" My brain is in overdrive, asking me over and over, *Why isn't Weston here, why isn't Weston here, why isn't Weston here?* I mean, not to be Captain Obvious here, but I *really* want to know why he's not here!

"Chosen ones for what?" Adam scratches his head, not getting my question.

Jenna sighs loudly and rolls her eyes. "Where is Weston?" she asks, cutting to the chase and pouting—and by the way, when Jenna pouts, she literally sticks her bottom lip out.

Derek's brow wrinkles, and I can't tell, but I think he's irritated. "I don't know, I'm not his babysitter. He's probably at home getting iced up and shit. Why do you even care, dude?"

"You did not just call me dude." Jenna is utterly affronted, and I just stand there watching the exchange with wide eyes.

Very entertaining.

"Why? Does it bother you, *dude*?" Yup, Derek is totally irritated. He and Jenna stare each other down until finally Jenna turns up her nose and stomps loudly out of the room.

Well, as loudly as someone can stomp in socks on a tile floor.

"What's *her* problem?" Adams asks, tossing his head at her retreating form.

"Yeah, what the hell," Derek adds. "What a bitch."

I snort. "Oh lord, where do you want me to start?" It would take me a year to explain all of Jenna's triggers for pissing her off (being called *dude* is apparently one of them), and we just don't have that kind of time.

I shake my head to get the fog out of my brain and let my hand lilt in the air. "Whatever. Anyway, let me get you to my dad's office. You're the last ones here."

After dropping Derek and Adam off, I shuffle off in my fuzzy slippers to find Jenna up in my room, lying flat on my bed with one hand holding open the latest issue of Teen Vogue, the other hand propping her chin up.

"Those are two of the *dumbest*-looking boys I have ever seen," she says without looking up as she flips a page of the magazine. I flop down beside her. "You should ask one of them out."

I pretend to think about it before I say, "Okay."

"What? Shut up, you slut!" she shouts, coming off the bed in a huff, magazine falling to the carpet. "I was *kidding!*"

I grab my stomach and fall over laughing. She's too easy.

"So was I, you moron. As if I would actually do that. Hockey players are like cavemen."

Jenna smirks. "I know *one* caveman I wouldn't mind dragging me around by the hair…"

"Honestly, Jenna. Why don't you just become his official stalker, for crying out loud? He's not a god. He's an athlete."

"Yeah, an athlete I'd let drag me around by the hair…"

I sit on the bed and bite down on my lower lip, debating. If I tell Jenna I caught Weston watching me in the library, at the lake, and again in the hallway, she will *freak*—not *just* freak, like, literally lose her mind. I would never hear the end of it on account of the big stalker crush she has on him.

On the other hand, if I *don't* tell her, I'll feel like I'm keeping a secret from her, which I have never done.

I go from biting my lip to biting my thumbnail.

Catching the nervous habit, Jenna homes in on me. "Wait, is there something you're not telling me? What's going on?" She studies me with her eyes narrowed suspiciously.

"Huh? What do you mean?"

"You're biting your nail. That means you're stressing out about something. Come on, tell Jenna what's wrong." Jenna plops back onto the bed with a flounce, sitting up against the headboard. She takes a pillow and settles it on her lap. "Here, lie down."

She pats the pillow, indicating I should lay my head on it.

I bite my lip, still debating.

"Just do it!" she hisses.

"God, you're pushy." I try to sound affronted.

"That's because you're a pushover. I battle for you."

"Yeah, you're a regular knight in shining armor," I mutter, but I move to lay my head down. Jenna starts braiding my hair and doesn't say anything.

She's waiting for me to say something.

I let out a long breath.

"Soooo…you know how I always make a big deal out of you mentally stalking Weston McGrath?"

Long pause, then, "*Duh.*"

"Well…there's been a development." Yeah, yeah, I know I'm being vague here, but I'm so nervous and am bracing myself for her reaction.

"*Yeah…*" I can feel Jenna holding her breath. She stops braiding my hair, and I wiggle my head around to encourage her to begin again. "Oh, hell no. I'm not doing your hair unless you talk, so spill—and this had better be good."

"He, um… Ugh." I can't get the words out. "A few days ago…he…"

"Spit it *out*, Molly!"

"A few days ago in the library, I caught him straight-up staring at me, staring at me hard—is that such a thing? Oh my god, then I caught him doing it in the hallway today before I smashed into Rick the Dick, so yeah, that's it." I blurt it all out in a long run-on sentence without taking a single breath.

The room is completely silent. Not even our cell phones interrupt with a text alert.

Neither of us are moving.

"Holy. Shit." Jenna has my braid suspended above my head, and she's staring down at me. Her eyes have gone huge. For a few minutes at least, she doesn't say anything else. It's taking all my focus not to fidget under her scrutiny. Finally, in a very low voice, she says, "Do you remember in eighth grade when we were playing Seven Minutes in Heaven and I got locked in with Kevin Dryer, and I not only let him make out with me but I also let him stick his hand up my shirt? I thought that was the best moment of my life."

"Um…" Where is she going with this?

"This is *so* much better than that."

***

I come back from grabbing snacks in the kitchen—correction: I come back from *sneaking* snacks in the kitchen—and Jenna is perched on the end of my bed, ready to pounce. The girl wants details and really only agreed to let me leave the room because I had to go to the bathroom. Otherwise I would have been held hostage.

This behavior, quite honestly, goes all the way back to middle school, back to when Jenna used to write this little column for the school newspaper. I think it was called *Seen and Heard in the Halls*, and it was basically a little gossip column. Of course she acted more like a reporter for the New York Times than for the Raven Middle School Gazette—even back then she took herself way too seriously.

"Okay, so, as you were saying, you were in the library, and you could feel him stripping you naked with his eyes." She has her fingertips folded into steeples, and they're pressing against her chin.

"No, that's *not* what I said. If you're going to twist everything around to make it sound tawdry, just forget it. I'm not telling you anything."

"All right! *All right*, I'll stop."

"Promise?"

"Yes, I pinky promise." She looks sincere, but with her it's so hard to tell. I take it one step further by screwing up my face and threatening her with a knuckle sandwich. It's too bad my fist looks so puny.

"I swear by all that is holy, Jenna, I don't mind if you say anything, but if you exaggerate or make shit up, I will tell your mom you took her Gucci purse to school the week she was on vacation, *and* that you spilled Pepsi on it during lunch *and* that you had to have it dry cleaned."

Jenna's skin blanches a little.

Her mom takes her designer bags *very* seriously.

"Molly! I *promise*. And you know what? Kudos to you for trying to blackmail me..." She tips her head to the side thoughtfully. "So, okay. What were you wearing in the library when he was eying you up?"

I set the pretzels I've been holding on the bed and crack open a sparkling water. It's lemon flavored and is apparently my mom's new favorite beverage, because there's a whole case of it in the pantry.

I take a sip then sputter, "Ugh, this is so gross! How do people drink it?"

Jenna snaps her fingers in front of my face. "Molly, the library. What were you wearing?"

"Huh? Oh. Um, I think I was wearing a jean skirt—the short one my mom hates—and my Boston Bruins T-shirt."

In case you're not up on your hockey trivia, the Bruins won themselves the Stanley Cup last year. Another interesting fact about me: *I am a closet hockey fan*. Now, before you start jumping down my throat, let me clarify, I am a fan of *professional* hockey, not the student-athlete variety. I won't bore you with the details, because it's common knowledge that my brother Matthew is a senior playing for the Wisconsin Badgers.

What's not common knowledge: my cousin Travis plays for the Pittsburgh Penguin, an NHL team. My parents have always been fanatics when it comes to hockey, but now that their nephew plays in the "big league" and their son plays for a Big Ten school, they're psycho about it.

It's not something I go around broadcasting, unless you count the team bumper stickers on my Jeep. Wait. I guess that *is* broadcasting it…

"Is that the hockey shirt you reworked to make it tighter?" Jenna's eyes are sparkling.

"Yup."

"Damn girl, I bet you looked hot as hell, especially to a guy like him. Man, I wish I had been there." She flops down backward and lays flat on her back, staring dreamily at the old Justin Bieber poster I have taped to the ceiling.

It's from fifth grade, okay?

"Maybe he was looking hard to see what my shirt said?"

"Or *maybe* he was just looking at your ta-tas," Jenna says. "Do you know how awesome it is that you had that shirt on? I mean, think about it. You've never been to a Ravens game, and here you are wearing a shirt from the NHL. I bet he got all hot and bothered—you know how eighteen-year-old guys are." She flips over to her stomach and reaches for the pretzels, popping two into her mouth at once. "He was probably wondering what the hell the deal was."

River Glen Ravens is the name of our high school athletics program, and yes I have been to a few of the games, but it has been a couple years. I think I was in eighth or ninth grade the last time I went to see my brother Matthew play.

"So what else were you wearing? What shoes did you have on?" Jenna takes the can of sparkling water I discarded and takes a healthy swig. "Wow, this really does taste like shit."

"I was wearing wedges, and I don't see why that really matters. Hey! I can't believe you don't remember any of this. I see you every day, and this was only a few days ago."

She shrugs. "I have my own issues I'm dealing with, okay?"

"Like…?"

"Like, *hello*, I can't find shoes to match my Fall Formal dress and it's driving me mental. Let's go to the mall in Clintonville this weekend. Maybe they'll have something." I watch her take another chug of the water before handing it to me. "Ugh, why are you letting me drink this? It's so shitty."

Taking the can, I set it on the bedside table, grinning.

Seriously, sometimes all you can do is laugh.

And that's just what we do—burst out laughing on my bed. Then I ask, "Why are you so worried about finding shoes? Fall Formal isn't for like, an entire month yet."

Jenna looks at me like I've sprouted two heads. "How can you *not* be worried about it? You haven't even found a *dress* yet."

"Well, that's an easy one. I don't have a date."

"That's your fault. *You* won't give anyone a chance."

"Honestly, Jenna, that's because all the guys I have to pick from act like jackasses, and you know how that drives me crazy. It's not exactly a crime to wait until I have a date to look at dresses. I'm okay not going."

"I don't even know you anymore," Jenna says in a staged whisper of mock horror.

"Seriously, how did I find you?" I ask, chuckling.

"I think you're remembering it all wrong. I totally found you. Now pass me that godawful water."

***

I am lying in bed, staring at my ceiling.

No matter how hard I try, it's impossible to fall asleep. It will not come to me.

Glancing at my clock, I note the time: 12:17 a.m. Groaning, I flop to my side and grab the iPod off my bedside table, put in the ear buds, and click to my "Mellow" playlist.

Letting out a long breath I hadn't realized I was holding in, I close my eyes and give in to what I've been fighting all day long: the image of Weston. The undeniable attraction I feel. The flutters I felt throughout my whole body when I caught him watching me.

And the ache in my heart that knows he's not the dating kind.

Molly

"My dog winks at me sometimes. I always wink back just in case it's some kind of code." – Derek Hanson

You might be thinking I spend every waking moment with Jenna—or any of my other friends—but in reality that's not the case.

Like today.

It's Saturday, and I'm standing in a stock room at the resort store where I work. The store serves several purposes. In the summer, it's a gift shop that sells collectibles with our town's logo on it. We also sell apparel, and some water sport accessories, like wakeboards and tubes. Then, during ski season, we sell winter apparel, skis, and snowboarding equipment.

I only work here so I can get a free season pass to the ski hill.

That, and my parents told me one afternoon when I

became a senior not to come home without a job, and this was literally the only place that was hiring.

The shop is located at the base of our mountain—which isn't actually a mountain but an old garbage landfill they turned into a ski hill—and in the winter, snowboarders and skiers can zip right up to the door if they need anything from the store, like glove warmers for example, or a funky new hat.

I work with one other girl from my school, Erin, and she is honestly a real pain in the butt. She's useless, and I'm almost positive her parents are friends with our manager because there is *no way* anyone would purposely hire her.

I'm still assessing her actual skillset.

Or lack thereof...

"Honestly, you are no help whatsoever," I mutter to Erin as I heave a cardboard box into the middle stock room with my foot. Yeah, it would be easier to bend down and push it, but today I'm feeling a little lazy myself. The store is pretty dead. Tourist traffic from the area's big lake hasn't turned into vacationers on a ski holiday just yet, so it's mostly just the occasional customer trickling in.

I glanced sideways at Erin, who is standing there watching me struggle with the box, offering me no assistance. I roll my eyes. "I can't believe they *pay* you."

"Ugh, I'm *so boredd*," she groans loudly, dragging out her sentence and leaning backward. She lets her arms fall limply to her side. "Ugh, I'm *dyinggg*. What time is it?"

"We still have almost two hours left," I say, irritated. I take the sharp cutter out of my apron and slice the heavy box open, careful not to cut into the merchandise inside—unlike that one time I cut into the box without thinking and ended up slicing a brand new ski coat right down the front.

That sucked.

I didn't have to pay for it or anything, but still.

"Who are you going to Fall Formal with this year?" Erin asks.

"I'm not."

"Not going? Or not having a date?" Really Erin? *Not having a date?* Way to pay attention in English class.

"I don't have a date, so technically I have no plans to go."

"So you don't have a dress?"

"Nope."

"Aww, that's so sad…" After she says this, I turn to face her and put my hand on my hip.

"Do I look sad to you?" I ask as Erin stares at me blankly. Okay, it's not blankly, exactly. She's actually looking at me like I'm a pitiful little critter. I let out a long sigh and ask, "Okay, well, who are *you* going to Fall Formal with?"

"Technically, he hasn't asked me yet, but I totally *know* he will…"

"Are you going to tell me or not, because we have stuff to do here."

"Derek Hanson. He winked at me yesterday."

"You think Derek Hanson is going to ask you to Fall Formal because he *winked* at you yesterday?"

"It was a suggestive wink with a lot of meaning. I could tell."

Really, what am I supposed to say to that? Suddenly, Erin claps her hands. "I know! Let's play a game!"

"Please, let's *not*."

Technically, she's supposed to be unloading a box of children's socks—you know, the kind that look all crazy and mismatched—but instead she's leaning up against a cleaning-supply shelf and peeling open a new pack of gum. Noisily, she dislodges a square from its foil and pops it into her mouth. "Wow, this is minty."

"You *do* know we have to get this done before tomorrow, don't you?" I ask, my question lingering in the air as it falls on deaf ears. Erin goes over to stand next to the stockroom door that separates the back storage area from the sales floor. She turns and grins. I can hear the chewing of her gum from the other side of the room. She sounds like my brother when he's gnawing away at a steak dinner.

Erin senses my sigh before I can even audibly get one out. "Calm down, would you?" (Wow, am I that predictable?) "It's not like you actually *need* this job if they fire you for not being productive." (Actually, Erin does have a point—that *is* technically true.) "So, like, here's what we're going to do, because if I don't do *something* fun I'm going to like, *die* of boredom."

"You could do some *work*." Ignoring me as usual, Erin pushes on.

"Okay, so like, the next guy that walks in that door, you have to—."

"No freaking way, Erin. *No!*"

"Okay, I'll do it then."

"Do what!" I damn near shout, exasperated.

"I'll flirt with the next guy who walks in that door,

even if he's, like, *super* old."

"That's the dumbest thing you've said all day. Plus, what if the next guy that walks in the door is a kid?"

"Well, if he's like, twelve, then that would like, totally make his *whole* year."

"Oh my god, you're so ridiculous…"

At that moment, the bell from the door jingles and I groan.

Lord help me.

I can hear the faint sound of Erin greeting the customers, and I resume unpacking the box of insulated Under Armour shirts that sits half empty on the floor. I look around for an available surface and remove a stack of resort maps. The shirts still have to be taken out of their clear plastic bags, put on hangers, and tagged.

Ugh, this is the part of the job that I hate.

Just then, my phone buzzes in the pocket of my apron.

Tasha: *How late do u work?*

Me: *Done in 2 hrs. Why?*

I slip the phone back into my pocket. It buzzes again almost immediately.

Tasha: *Scrimmage starts in 20 min.*

She's talking about the hockey preseason scrimmage the Ravens have this afternoon against the prep school in a nearby city, and Tasha just happens to be dating a guy from their team.

Me: *There's no way I'll make it. It'll b over long b4 i get done if it's just a scrimmage.*

Tasha: *Ok. Will save seat just in case.*

Me: *thx.*

I know there's no way I'll make it, and really no way I'd go even if I could. Besides, what I want hardly matters since I'm stuck here at work until my shift ends.

For the next two hours, I stay in the back room and unpack boxes of shirts, socks, and even a box of ski masks. Since it's getting closer to October, the weather might be warm enough to sit at the lake for the day, but ski season will be upon us in a matter of weeks. Erin doesn't help at all, of course, instead staying up front and accosting the few customers that actually wander in. One couple comes in to pre-order ski jackets, and some poor random man comes in to pick up the snowboard bindings he had tightened. I'm really grateful I wasn't up front for *that* little exchange if Erin's still playing her "boredom buster".

By the time five rolls around, my stomach is growling.

I text Jenna

Me: *I'm starving.*

Stuffing the phone in my messenger bag, I head out to my Jeep and sit waiting in the parking lot at the base of the grassy ski hill. I haven't even put the key in the ignition yet, because if Jenna texts me back and wants to grab something to eat with me, then I'll have to turn an entirely different direction once I get out of the parking lot.

So I wait.

My phone buzzes.

Jenna: *We literally just ate. Still at Mcdonalds. Want me to grab something with you anyway?*

Me: *No worries, running to grab mongolian, it's been an age.*

Jenna: *No value menu? One dollar, hollar!*

Me: *I'll just go sit in a corner somewhere, alone...*

Jenna: *Don't talk to any perverts.*

Me: *Darn I was planning on it.*

Sighing, I start my ignition and quickly lean over to feel around inside my bag to see if there's a book I can read while sitting at the restaurant. Kyoto Grill is one of my new favorite places to eat. Basically, you build your own stir-fry and slap everything you picked out to eat onto a five-hundred-degree stone. The only problem I have is the bowl they give you to fill is *never* big enough! I have to pile all the ingredients on my bowl until it resembles a mini-mountain. Then, my vegetables always topple off before I make it to the chef, and that's pretty embarrassing, but the food is fantastic, not to mention healthy, and since the place is relatively new, it's never crowded.

On a few occasions, I've been the only patron there.

About twenty-five minutes later, I'm all set in a corner booth at Kyoto with a steaming hot plate of stir-fry, a somewhat racy teen romance (that Jenna lent me, of course), and my iPod. I set my phone on the table and put in my ear buds, deciding that maybe a low-key playlist would be best. After all, I can't really read if I've got Drake blasting in my ears.

I take a few bites of my dinner, which is a combination of noodles and vegetables that taste amazing, and open my book to the earmarked page. I don't read very often, but this book has managed to keep my interest. Then again, give me the name of one teenage girl who can resist a story about a good girl secretly crushing on the school's bad boy... Clever girl that I am, the irony isn't lost on me.

My phone buzzes.

Jenna: *Find a pervert with a long noodle?*

Me: *Lol. Leave me alone I'm eating.*

Jenna: *Don't choke. And text me so I know you survived.*

Me: *Yes mom :p*

Jenna: *Don't talk to stranglers.*

Jenna: *Dammit autocorrect! *strangers.*

Giggling, I stuff my mouth with a forkful of rice noodles. They're so delicious I close my eyes and moan out loud—every bite is totally worth the torture of a day spent working with Erin. In my opinion, it's a reward that's been truly earned, and I mean to savor it.

As I start a new chapter in my book, the steady stream of music pumps from my iPod, through my ear buds and into my ears. I casually bop along to the rhythm of "(Kissed You) Good Night" by Gloriana. I just can*not* get enough of this romantic, playful song, even though it's an older one. I'm the type of person who, when they really like a tune, listens to it over and over, and that's why I've listened to this one, *oh*, about a thousand times.

I adjust the volume on my iPod, turning it down a tad. It's at that moment that I look up and almost choke on my food.

Standing in the entry of the dining room, holding a plate of his own, is Weston. I can't figure out if he's some figment of my imagination I've conjured up because I can't stop thinking about him, or if he's really standing there. I almost rub my eyes in disbelief but stop myself.

Unfortunately, I'm not hallucinating.

Fortunately, I don't think he sees me yet, so I slouch down and hold my book up in front of my face, hoping to conceal the fact that I'm both chewing and swallowing frantically. Why does this damn book have a young couple holding hands on the cover of it? *Curse* Jenna and her smut.

I literally have noodles hanging from my mouth, and I can't suck them in fast enough.

Shit, shit, double shit. This is humiliating.

Well, it's not like I've never been humiliated before. I mean, I could tell you about the one time on April Fool's Day a few years back when Jenna cut boob holes in the front of my gym shirt. Yes, it was just like Regina George from *Mean Girls*, but *ugh*! Never mind. That is so not my point here.

"Hey. Mind if I keep you company?"

Please god let the earth just open up and swallow me whole, I pray, *like, as in* right *freaking now. Seriously.*

I look up to see Weston standing there in his masculine glory, staring down at me with expectation in his eyes, one hand holding his dinner and one hand stuffed in the pocket of his black Adidas athletic pants. His hair is wet, presumably from the shower he took after his game.

There is a red gash in his bottom lip that's obviously new.

Holy shit is it hot.

Stop staring at his lips, Molly. Stop it.

I must hesitate for too long, because those amazing lips hitch up into a small smile and he shrugs. "It's cool. I didn't mean to bother you." He says the words but makes no effort to walk away.

"No, no. It's fine. You surprised me, that's all." I shut the book, slam it down, and push it upside down to the corner of the table. "I usually have the place to myself."

"Yeah?" That one uttered word has a lilt to it that sends heat racing through parts of my body that have long been dormant. I resist the urge to visibly shiver as I invite him to share my booth.

"Yeah. Here, sit."

Weston slides into the booth with a grace you wouldn't expect from a guy his size. Setting his plate down, he unrolls his utensils from the paper napkin and places his fork on the left side of the plate, knife on the right. He shocks me even further by laying the napkin across one knee.

My, my, such good table manners.

He clears his throat then says, "I don't think we've ever really been introduced. I'm Wes." He's holding his hand across the table for me to shake, and I stare at it like he intends to shock me with a Taser. Large and calloused, this is the hand of a guy who's seen his share of hard work.

I unintentionally slide my hand slowly into his palm, sending a ripple of sensations through my body. His hand is steady and warm, and suddenly I'm in no rush to leave.

"I'm Molly." My voice is soft, just above a whisper.

"Hi, Molly." His voice is like satin sliding across my skin.

Say my name again, please...just once more...

I don't think I've ever met a boy with a voice this baritone and erotic. Take Bryan Bossner for example. At seventeen years old, his voice still cracks when he's shouting in gym class. Suddenly, it makes more sense to me why girls always seem to be fawning over Weston McGrath.

It's not because of the hockey, and it's not because he's so damn good-looking. Nope. It's because his voice could charm the pants off a nun.

I mean, if nuns *wore* pants.

Finally releasing my hand, Weston points at his ears. "What are you listening to?" He is already digging into his pasta, which has steam rising from it.

"Huh? Oh my gosh!" How rude of me! I quickly remove my ear buds and wind them around my iPod, setting them on top of my book.

He chuckles, low and deep in his chest, and I can't help it—I shiver.

"Cold?"

Oh my god, shoot me now.

"Um, sort of. I left my sweater in the car." To validate my lie, I rub my hands up and down my arms a few times and say, "*Brrr.*"

I am such an idiot. The action must have drawn Weston's attention to my shirt, which is a navy tee bearing the logo of the resort where I work. He raises his eyebrows.

"You work at Mount Olympia?"

I nod. "Yup. In the gift shop. Nothing all that exciting, but I do get a free lift ticket every season, so…"

"No shit. You board?"

"Why, do you consider yourself *boring*?" I tease.

He screws his face up and looks at me like I've lost my mind. "No, Molly, I meant do you snowboard."

Seriously, *I am a complete idiot.*

"Um, no. I ski, actually. What about you?"

"Yeah, I board, though not as much as I used to because of, you know, hockey."

I nod in understanding. "I can imagine you're crazy busy."

Across from me, Weston starts fiddling with his fork, pushing a few noodles around on his plate. He looks at me directly, and what comes out of his mouth next genuinely dumbfounds me. "Look, Molly, about the other day at school…I…" He pauses and lets out a long breath. "I can't stop thinking about how Rick treated you, and…well, I'm sorry. I'm sorry I didn't step in and tell him to shove off. He's an asshole and you seemed really…" He searches for a word. "Kind of scared."

I process this information. "It's okay. I mean, yeah, I was a little freaked out, but…I survived." I feel like I'm stumbling over my words.

"Well, if you want me to beat the crap out of him for you, I will." He smiles and we both laugh.

"I can see the headlines now: 'Local guy gets butt kicked for…*acting like a guy*.'"

"Ah, come on, Molly. We're not *all* complete assholes."

Weston

"You talk cute." (What I want to say when Molly is speaking) – Weston

As I'm saying the words, '*We're not all complete assholes,*' Molly's bright green eyes get real wide, and she gives me this dubious stare like she doesn't believe a word coming out of my mouth…which I guess makes sense, because sometimes even *I* don't believe a word coming out of my mouth.

We guys *are* kind of all assholes.

It's not like it's a big secret. Even so, I'm not going to admit that out loud.

I stare at Molly for a few seconds.

I can't help it; I really can't—she's just so goddamn adorable. As I wonder why she's single, she gets quiet and her cheeks start getting a little red. Her fork hovers over her plate, and I think she's about to say something in protest. Instead she shrugs, nodding slowly. "Yeah, okay. Maybe you're not."

Ah shit, she has freckles across her nose, the kind you want to lean in and kiss one by one.

How cute is that?

"You can't judge us all because one guy treated you like shit, right?"

"So you're saying you're not an asshole?" Molly tips her head, looks at me, and lazily starts to trail her fork around her plate, pushing noodles this way and that. She rests her chin in the palm of her other hand with a small smile on her face, and I notice she has the shadow of a dimple in her right cheek. "All right. I believe you."

7

Molly

"Once I walked in on my brother belting out the words to a Hannah Montana song. The person who said, 'No one looks stupid when they're having fun,' was a liar. Charlie looked like an idiot." – Ella Beauchamp, soccer teammate

"So really, what were you listening to?" Weston asks again.

"You're not just going to sit quietly and let me eat, are you?"

His response is to laugh out loud. The sound is crazy wonderful—low, rich, and vibrating deep within his chest, his very...*muscular* chest. I preen with the satisfaction that I've made this god-like teenager laugh, knowing it's because I've surprised him with my bluntness.

I huff a sigh for show before answering and trying to swallow my embarrassment. "You've probably never heard of it."

"Try me." He leans forward, flexes his biceps, and slowly begins twirling some noodles around his fork...

stabs a few vegetables…takes a large bite. A lock of hair falls in his eyes.

He doesn't bother brushing it away.

And yeah, I totally want to do it for him.

"You don't seem like the type of guy who enjoys romantic girly songs." I give him a sideways glance, eying him skeptically.

He considers this then nods his head. "You would be correct, but *now* inquiring minds want to know—just what is on that iPod of yours, Molly Wakefield?"

Dear Lord, he's teasing me and I *love* it.

Love it, love it.

I love that he keeps saying my name. It's not just the *way* he's saying my name, but the simple fact that it's on his lips! I love the way his mouth moves when he's talking, his battered bottom lip going slightly crooked when he smiles, and how his voice gets animated when he's being playful.

I suddenly find myself developing a titanic-sized crush on him. It's instantaneous, like a bucket of cold reality that has just come crashing down on my head.

I clear my throat. "Okay, fine, but after I tell you, let's eat. I'm starving, and you're already one step ahead of me." I point to his half-eaten plate of food with my fork; meanwhile, I've barely touched mine. I can tell he's amused, and I wonder where all this bravado on my part is coming from.

However, in this situation, it's best to play it cool.

With a guy like Weston McGrath—a guy who has groupies—the only females who are going to stand out are those who can resist him. Give him a challenge. Play hard to get.

Weston eyes my food thoughtfully and points to my plate. "Just so you know, anything you don't eat by the time I'm done with *my* food, I'm going to try to steal." He says this very matter-of-factly.

"That's the best you've got? You're only going to *try* to steal it?" As these coy words are rolling off my tongue, my eyes drift. I notice that one of his bottom teeth is chipped, and my eyes linger once again on that cut on his lip. It's swollen, and there is dry blood in the corner of his mouth.

Without realizing it, my tongue darts out and I run it slowly over my bottom lip.

He studies me with his head cocked and doesn't say anything for a few heartbeats.

He shakes his head and blinks. "So…the song you were listening to…"

His persistence is irritating—and also incredibly adorable.

"I'm beginning to feel like this is a battle of wills." I set down my fork. "Fine, you big baby. I'll tell you, but you probably won't know it." I finger the tablecloth and feel my face getting hot.

I know what you're thinking: *Why is she making this such a big deal?* Um, because I'm listening to a song about love and kissing and now he wants me to blurt it out. I don't want him to get the wrong idea. Well, a perverse part of me does…the part that wants to stand up, walk over to his side of the booth, and crawl onto his lap.

Holy crap, where did that come from? I'm not sure how I feel about this saucy Molly Wakefield taking control of my body.

Newsflash: my hormones seem to have kicked in and are full-fledged raging. Well, I better cool it down, because despite his intensity, he's not even really flirting.

Inhaling, I quickly blurt out, "Youshouldhavekissedme."

"What? Wait. *What?*" His eyebrows shoot up into his shaggy hairline and the play of expressions on his gorgeous face is priceless. It ranges somewhere between *I can't believe my luck* and *Get me the hell out of here.*

I laugh. "The song is called 'You Should Have Kissed Me'. It's by Gloriana. Seriously, get your mind out of the gutter." Actually, the name of the song is "(Kissed You) Good Night", but I don't mention liking my title for the song better as I twirl some noodles around my fork and blow on them.

"I hate to break it to you, Molly, but my mind is pretty deep in the gutter." Weston winks at me. "I dumped it back there on my way into the building."

He winks again.

Okay. Definitely flirting.

Do people still swoon, or am I laying on the drama a little too heavily? Because dear Lord, right now I could pass out and die.

Then I have this sudden random thought: if I were delusional, like Erin from work, that wink would constitute an invitation to the Fall Formal dance. I almost giggle out loud at the thought but catch myself and just do a generic eye roll instead.

"So wait, wait, wait—the song is about making out?" Weston stuffs more noodles into his face and waggles his eyebrows. "Tell me more."

"Yes. *No*... It's basically about..." I pause to think about this and screw my face up in thought. "Hmm...it's basically about a girl arriving home from a date that she *thought* went great, but her date doesn't kiss her goodnight, and naturally she wonders why."

"Naturally," Weston interjects airily.

I ignore him and continue, warming up to my topic. "The girl watches him through her curtains as he sits in his car. He can't decide if he should go back or not, but then he finally runs back up to the house."

"And then what? They make out?" He sounds like an excited little kid, and at the same time I can feel him looking at my lips. The scrutiny is intense, and I resist the urge to lick them again.

I'm tempted—*so* very tempted—just to see what would happen.

"Well, *yeah*, I guess. But not like that..."

He puts down his fork and stares at me. "Okay. Like how, then?"

He's completely serious.

I wave my hand around in the air, trying to conjure up an explanation. No words come out. I cannot believe I'm having this conversation with Weston McGrath, *of all people*, and the very first time we formally meet to boot.

"Look, just forget it."

"Hell no I won't forget it! Are you *trying* to drive me nuts? You know what? Here, give me your iPod. I'll just listen to it myself." He doesn't wait for me to hand it to him. Nope. The brute leans across the table and snatches the iPod, which is dwarfed by his large hands.

His bare arms are tan, toned, and now that we're sitting here and he's distracted, I can openly study his tattoo. It's an intricate design that starts in the middle of his forearm and ends at his muscular shoulder blade. It looks like it might actually end even farther under his shirt—like maybe his collarbone—but from where I'm sitting, it's hard to tell. I can definitely make out a few objects: a raven (our school mascot), a crucifix, and a girl's name (Zoe, I think?) all woven into a tapestry of Celtic designs. It is entirely black.

Weston has my ear buds in and is adjusting the volume of my pink Nano.

I can tell that the song is on because his eyes settle on mine.

You should have kissed me, such a wistful and romantic song. Even though I can't hear the song playing, I can hear the words and rhythm playing in my head: *I should have kissed you, I should have pushed you up against the wall, I should have kissed you, just like I wasn't scared at all.*

Dear Lord, I wonder what he's thinking.

Weston is watching me watch him, his dark chocolate eyes hooded as if he's gotten sleepy. His dark, inky eyelashes are sinfully long for a guy.

Minutes tick by.

Slowly—causing me anguish—he runs his tongue several times over the cut on his lower lip before reaching up and removing the ear buds.

I can't stand it. I have to ask.

"So…?" *What did you think,* my mind is screaming.

He thinks for a heartbeat then gives me an uncommitted, "You're right, I've never heard it."

Wait. *What?*

That's it? After all that buildup? Okay, so obviously the buildup was only on my end, but in any case, I feel disappointment. *Really, Molly, what did you expect?* He's a *guy*.

All this talk about kissing has me hot and bothered. For real, I wouldn't fight him off if he suddenly decided to ravish me with kisses. After all, I haven't been kissed in ages, and I've almost forgotten what it feels like. I'm not really sure what to say at this point, so I just continue eating my half-eaten meal, which has gotten cold during our conversation.

I rack my ravaged brain for a safe topic. "So, Weston, how did the scrimmage go today?"

There. Safe enough.

His eyebrows shoot up. "You weren't there?" he says and stops chewing. Obviously he's surprised; I can tell by the look on his face.

On second thought, maybe *not* such a safe topic...

"I was *working*, but...I usually don't go to the games, no." I can see by his confused expression that this is a foreign concept. He tips his head to the side, like a cocker spaniel. A girl not following his every move? Shocking! "Why do you seem so surprised?"

"Why not?" he asks. His plate is completely empty, so he picks up his glass of water, picks out the straw and, tipping his head back, chugs it downs.

I can't help but admire the muscles of his collarbone and the smooth area of skin just visible above the V-neck of the raggedy T-shirt.

He sets his glass down with a loud *thunk*, and the abrupt sound snaps me out of my perusal.

"Why not what?" *Earth to Molly.*

"Why do you usually not come to the games?"

I shrug. "I just…don't. I just don't think they're that big a deal."

Weston's dark eyes bore into me like I've just delivered an insult. I can tell he's fighting back a sarcastic remark, because the muscles in his clenched jaw tick. "Not a big deal?"

I study him for a moment. His nostrils flare.

Testosterone much?

"You want the truth? Here it is: I prefer watching the NHL."

Weston snorts his obvious skepticism with a laugh.

Setting my napkin on the table, I lean forward onto my elbows and point to his mouth. I'm about to go in for the kill. "So…did you get that gash on your lip from a high stick, or…did some left wing run interference when you tried to light the lamp?"

Causally, I lean back and wait. (For you non-hockey-lovers, I just asked him if he got nailed by someone's stick while trying to score a goal).

Weston blinks.

Then he blinks again.

Okay, at this point you're probably thinking to yourself, *What's he gonna say, what's he gonna do*, and you wouldn't be alone, because I'm wondering too—but here's the thing: I don't stick around to find out.

***

An old actress from the 1900s named Mae West once said, "When a girl goes bad, men go right after her." I read that quote once in Cosmo magazine and loved it so much I tore the page out and pinned it to the only space in my room where I'm allowed to hang things on my wall: a large bulletin board next to my desk.

On the weekends, when Jenna and Tasha (or any of our other friends) aren't with their boyfriends, one thing we've always loved to do is sit and read old back issues of magazines. In fact, we've been doing this for so many years, I happen to keep a laundry basket of old magazines in the back of my closet, which my mom has tried to throw out on numerous occasions. You know how it is.

To be honest, most times I read Cosmo—or any other magazine targeted toward, let's face it, woman in their twenties—very little applies to me. For example:

1. I don't need fifty sex tips to drive a man wild, because, well, I'm not having any.
2. I don't need to know how to wear hair extensions without looking like I have Barbie Doll hair.
3. And I *certainly* don't need the boyfriend quizzes, because as we all know, I don't have one.

Anyway, the Mae West quote has been hanging on my pin board for months and months now, and sometimes when I'm doing my homework, I'll glance up and read it. There have even been times it's inspired me to go after things I want—not necessarily guys, but other things too, like class officer (I'm vice president). Basically that short, sassy sentence has taught me not to be such a wimp.

So here I am, halfway to my car in the parking lot of Kyoto Grill, when Weston McGrath—the boy everyone claims is such a hard-ass he won't even date—comes chasing out after me.

Just like I suspected he would.

Like I hoped he would.

"Molly, stop! Where are you going?" He catches up and steps into stride beside me. I continue walking, my car just a few yards away.

I let out the breath I've been holding. "Look, I didn't mean to insult you back there. I'm sorry."

"Is that what this is all about?"

Um, no actually, I got up purposely to see if you'd follow me.

And you did.

It's gotten dark out, and the parking lot lamps are glowing above us. There are only a few vehicles present, one of them a lime green Kawasaki crotch rocket. "That must be yours, huh? I wouldn't have taken you for a green guy—blue seems to be more your color."

"Yeah, well, I let my little sister pick out the color. I'm always getting a rash of shit about it from the guys, so… yeah." He runs his tan fingers through his hair. All at once I'm aware of Weston in a completely different way—as a sensitive older brother.

"How old is she?"

"Are you trying to change the subject?"

I laugh. "Yes. Are you going to let me?" Since I have no idea what to say, I start digging for my keys as we approach my Jeep. Weston walks over and leans his shoulder against it, watching me with his arms crossed. Glancing up, I wonder if he owns any shirts with sleeves. Under the lamp light, the contours of his jaw and the angles of his arms are more defined, and his eyes look black.

Ugh, Weston is so handsome my heart beats fast within my chest.

Only the sound of cars driving by fills the air. Then, *finally*, those noises are joined by the jingle of my car keys.

"My sister's name is Kendall. She's eleven."

"Has she ever been on that thing?"

"Hell no, I'd never take her on it—not that my parents would actually let me. Once she begged me to drive her around the cul-de-sac in our subdivision, but…" He shrugs. "Besides, I'd feel horrible if anything ever happened while she was on the back of it."

"I don't blame you. Those things can be scary." *And sexy as hell.*

"Yeah, they can be if the driver isn't careful. My parents made me take a few extra safety classes, so…" He shrugs again.

"So you're a safe driver?"

"More like a responsible driver. I've never had a passenger, and I'm not like some of those assholes who rev their engines. Bikes don't have to be so damn loud, you know." He pauses. "So you know, I'm dying to ask…" Weston's sentence trails off, the low timbre of his voice filling the air.

I suppose I could pretend not to know what he's talking about—after all, feigning ignorance happens to be a talent of mine, a craft honed through years of lying for my idiot brother. Yes, Matthew paid me; I consider lying for him one of my first paying jobs. Weston wants to know where all that hockey jargon came from, and if I actually know what any of it means.

Can't say I blame him.

"You know, I kind of want to hear you ask…" I tease. *Because the sound of your voice is giving me goose bumps and makes me tingle.*

I enjoy teasing him, and truthfully, I could very well stand and literally listen to him talk all night. Here in this dimly lit parking lot, it feels like we are the only two people around. Maybe it's just me, but the air has a…crackle, and it definitely feels intimate, almost like there's tangible anticipation stirring the air around us.

I rest my back against the door of the Jeep so we're leaning side by side, and I gaze up at the pitch-black sky, watching for a shooting star. River Glen is mostly rural—the town isn't even considered a suburb of Chicago, which is over an hour away—so on a clear night like tonight, the sky is crystal clear and perfect for stargazing, no smog from the city to block the view.

"Okay. I'll bite. Where the hell did that come from back there?"

I turn my head to face him and laugh out loud. "Is Mr. Big Bad Hockey Captain impressed?"

"Shit yeah."

Good, the voices inside my head scream.

"Hmm, well, since you asked so nicely…my brother plays for Madison and…my cousin is Travis Locke…of the Bruins."

The Bruins won the Stanley Cup last year—and in case you didn't know, the Stanley Cup is like the Super Bowl of Hockey."

Weston lets out a low whistle and looks at me with a new kind of interest—shocked, excited, and little bit predatory. He shakes his head slowly. "How did I not know this?"

I shrug. "Well, Matthew is five years older, so we would have only been in eighth grade when he was a freshman at Madison. Technically he's a fifth-year senior now, so it's his last year playing."

"I've actually heard of him. He's awesome. And Travis Locke is your cousin?" He lets out another whistle through those full lips. His eyes are brilliant. "Wow," he says slowly. "So…wow. You actually know what you're talking about?" Unexpectedly, he braces himself against the Jeep with both arms steadied against the cold metal on either side of my head. His face is bent mere inches from mine. *Just a little closer, Weston, come on…* "Or do you just have a few things memorized for show?"

"You *still* don't believe I know what I'm talking about?" I force the question out in a soft whisper, a lump forming in my throat as his face inches closer.

He whispers back, "Maybe you just don't seem like the type."

Gasp! How dare he use my own words against me? Outrageous!

I'm giddy.

The gauntlet has been thrown, the challenge accepted. I draw my next sentence out slowly. "Oh, really…so what type *am* I?"

Weston draws closer still, and now I can feel his breath on my face.

It's warm and minty. Funny, I don't remember him chewing on a mint...

He is so close that as my eyes scan his face, I notice a small scar in the corner of his left eyebrow...one on the bridge of his nose...another on his chin. Stubble darkens his jaw. Instinctively, my hands want to cradle the hard lines of his face. He's making me want to push him up against the light post and maul him. In a parking lot.

I inhale. He smells like soap and aftershave.

Weston cocks his eyebrow and chews on his lower lip in thought. I see the wheels turning in his head. "Okay. What are the walls surrounding the ice rink called?"

I roll my eyes and look off into the distance. "Pfft. Please, don't insult me. They're called the boards."

He gives an undignified snort. "All right, that was beginner's luck. Anyone could've gotten that one."

"Beginner's luck? Really, Weston?" I sass him. "If you're going to discount my answer, then why did you ask?"

He eyes roam my face and land on my lips as he says, "Change on the fly."

My legs are a little wobbly now, like jelly, but I manage to roll my eyes again and sigh. "Substituting a player during the game." Is that my voice shaking? I can't tell, but I pray that it's not.

We stay this way, Weston hovering over me, his large capable hands framing my head on the cold metal of my car. The only sound between us is our labored breathing. It's like he can't make his mind up about whether to go all the way or pull back. And I...have never wanted a kiss so badly in my entire life.

Something is holding him back, and his face backs away slowly.

Finally, Weston whispers, "Damn."

Yeah, exactly.

Damn.

Molly

8

"Shut. Up. You can quote me on that." – Jenna

"Wait a minute, wait a minute, wait a minute—start over. Are you telling me Weston McGrath sat and ate a *meal* with you? And you didn't pass out and die? Oh em gee, I would have choked and *died* right there on the spot. Fainted *dead* away." Jenna is sitting at my desk, straddling the chair and staring holes into me with her intensity. She was my first phone call as I left the Kyoto Grill parking lot.

And, of course, she insisted on coming straight over.

She pounced on me as soon as I walked into the house and hasn't stopped talking since.

I shift uncomfortably under her scrutiny. I'm not good with all the attention on me. "Well, I *almost* did, so what does that tell you."

"Okay, so you're sitting there enjoying your noodles,

when..." Jenna doesn't let up, waving her hand in the air in a way that means *go on*. She wants me to relive every detail, over and over. Honestly, I've told her all this already.

Every...wonderful...delicious...detail.

But, being the good friend I am, I indulge her.

Again.

"So. I'm sitting there, and when I look up, *there he is*."

"Shut up."

"*Yes*." I'm being very dramatic, and she is loving it. "Then he walks over and asks if he can sit down. He said, and I quote, 'Mind if I keep you company?' And who am I to deny him?"

"As if you would!"

"So then I forgot I had my iPod on—"

"Was he a jerk?" Jenna interrupts, leaning forward, tipping the chair up on its front legs. I bite my lip and gaze at it nervously. She is *so* going to fall, or the chair legs are going to break off—either way, not good.

"No. He was..." *Dreamy*. "Nice. It was pleasant."

"Ew. Nice is boring. Was he coming on to you? Did he flirt?"

"Nice isn't boring, Jenna. We had fun." *Actually, I wanted to climb into his lap.*

"You know what, Molly? I live for this shit. The least you can do is *humor* me, for crying out loud. Give me *something*! Anything! Don't use words like 'nice' and 'fun'!" She throws her arms in the air, exasperated.

My phone beeps.

Picking it up, a number pops up onto my screen that I don't recognize, but I immediately know who it's from.

I think my heart just stopped.

212-555-9083: *Are you coming to my game this week?*

How on Earth did Weston get my number? I look up at Jenna, who is staring at me expectantly.

I swallow hard.

"Why do you look like you just crapped your pants?" she asks crassly. Hey, I didn't say she was my *classiest* friend.

"Er..." Suddenly, Jenna is jumping—no, *tripping*—off the chair and bouncing on the bed next to me. The chair actually falls and hits the desk, toppling unceremoniously and landing on its side. She snatches my phone up and begins shrieking.

"Holy shit! Holy shit, Molly! Weston McGrath has the *hots* for you! For you, my best friend!" She clutches the phone to her chest and squeals.

Loudly.

"Shhh, shhh! Oh my god, be quiet, will you?" I'm hissing at her now, but she couldn't care less. She carries on like One Direction has just walked into the room. I keep shushing her. "Jenna, shut up before my parents hear you."

"You have to respond." She gasps. "Put 'Hell yeah, baby,' and then—"

I start laughing because she's actually being serious.

She is always making me laugh. "Give me the damn phone back, you freak." I sit there, biting my lip. Wait... what *do* I want to say? After thinking about it for a few more seconds and swatting Jenna away several times, I start typing.

Me: *I would consider it…but I don't even know who this is*

There. That sounds flirty but not too enthusiastic.

"Why did you put that!" Jenna shouts, flapping her arms in exasperation. "You should just tell him you're going! Ugh, you're so going to ruin this, I just know it," she accuses, pacing around my room like a caged tiger.

My phone dings again.

212-555-9083: *You know who this is.*

Me: *I do? Weird. I don't recognize this number*

212-555-9083: *You come to my game and I'll score a goal for you.*

Me: *(rolling my eyes) One goal? I *might* get out of bed for a hat trick*

"Oh my god, why would you say that? What's a hat trick? You are such a weirdo! Program him into your phone already, would you? This is driving me nuts!"

"*You* are driving *me* nuts," I say to her. My stomach is in knots and my hands are actually sweating—sweating, if you can believe it. Ugh, gross. "A hat trick is a hockey term, *Jenna*. It means one person scores three goals in one game."

Duh.

I am so nervous. I click on Weston's phone number, quickly adding him to my contacts.

About fifteen torturous minutes go by before he responds. Doesn't he know how rude it is to keep a girl waiting like that?

Weston: *I'll see what i can do*

Well then.

Weston

> "If you weren't such a douche, maybe you'd score off the ice too." – random jackass

I can't help but wonder if she'll show up.

So far, after scanning the crowd like a whipped puppy, I haven't caught sight of her, and believe me, I've been watching.

I am standing in the sin-bin—otherwise known as the penalty box—for hooking an opposing player with my stick, and I take the opportunity to remove my helmet. The reprieve is only two minutes, but it's giving me back the energy I need to get back in the game.

My hair is sticking to my forehead from the sweat dripping down it, and there is blood on my tongue. The gash in the corner of my mouth must have torn when my opponent elbowed me in the chin—the same player who was talking trash during the face-off at the beginning of the game.

Which is pretty typical, actually.

But still. The little prick.

I reach up and wipe the blood away with the heel of my palm before strapping my helmet back on. I look up in the stands and see my mom pumping her fists at the action on the ice. She's waving a giant foam finger and her River Glen High sweatshirt has my button on it.

Jeez, Mom.

My dad, on the other hand, is sitting quietly to her right. His arms are crossed and he's leaning forward. From here, I can see that his eyebrows are furrowed and his hard features are set in a rigid line. He has a dark mustache framing most of his mouth, which my mom hates, but I know he's frowning nevertheless.

Nothing new there.

I get my passion for hockey from him; he used to play for Illinois University. Dad never had any desire to turn pro or pursue it after college, but he was my coach growing up, back when I was in the pee-wee league—although there was never anything remotely 'pee-wee' about me.

Okay, fine.

When I was younger I was mostly 'husky', but we won't get into *those* details. Dad bought me my first set of real blades when I was around four years old, and that was also the first winter he froze a slab of ice in our backyard and taught me how to skate.

I was a natural.

The sirens go off on the rink. River Glen has scored another goal while I'm in the penalty box. To get my head back in the game and out of my ass, I begin striking the door to the penalty box with my stick in a steady rhythm.

The plexi-glass is the only thing keeping me off that ice.

There are only twenty-five more seconds left to stand here behind this gate.

I've already scored one goal tonight, and we've only been playing fifteen minutes. That leaves me forty-five more minutes to score another two.

Then I'll have my hat trick.

Molly

I know the second he spots me. I can *feel* it.

Even though I'm wearing a ball cap with my hair pulled back into a ponytail, he instinctually knows I've arrived, just as I instinctually know he's watching me without having to actually see it.

Shit. Shouldn't he be focusing on the game?

I'm totally late too, and maybe if I hadn't arrived between the second and third periods, I could have come and gone without being noticed *at all*. Another issue is that I'm with Jenna and, never the shrinking violet, she's decked out in an eye-popping hot-pink jean jacket. Her long blonde hair is thrown into a messy top knot, and she's wrapped her head with an aqua scarf.

You would literally have to be *blind* to miss her.

Not to mention, she's balancing a large popcorn and soda—yup, just like we're headed to a movie—in her hands, all while teetering on platform sandals. You wouldn't *think* there would be concessions at a high school hockey game, but oh! That's where you'd be wrong, and Jenna just loves her some popcorn. On the bright side, at least with this throng I won't have to listen to her crunching like I do at the movies.

She's a really loud popcorn eater.

We find a large group of our friends and shimmy across the bleachers, over through the crowd. Down on the rink, our players are gathered against the boards while Coach Callahan barks at them as they stand in an assembly of panting, padding, and sweat. Even so, it's not difficult to miss the penetrating black eyes seeking out mine.

Weston wiggles his eyebrows at me.

Maybe I'm just being paranoid, but I feel a hundred heads turn to see who he made the gesture at, and my face lights on fire. Whispering and some pointing from within the crowd immediately follow. *Real subtle, Weston. Thanks.*

As I'm glancing around the stadium, I catch sight of a woman—the foam finger on her hand is really hard to miss, and she's obviously a mom with her school sweatshirt and spirit gear—and after Weston makes eyes at me from the ice, she snaps around in her bleacher seat. I watch her watch me as I spread a fleece blanket out onto the small section of stadium seating next to Jenna. Surprisingly, this woman also appears to be studying me back, and I shift awkwardly under her open examination, finally unable to take the scrutiny.

I break the brief connection and plop my butt down onto the bench.

All this gazing and staring is really making me feel foolish.

Everyone—both students and parents—begin to cheer wildly as our team reenters the ice for the third, and last, period. Ahead by two points, this should be an easy victory.

"They are kicking ass!" one of our guy friends shouts to me over the noise. "McGrath has scored two goals! Two!" He holds up two fingers to demonstrate.

"Gee, thanks Marcus, we couldn't figure that one out by ourselves," Jenna shouts at him teasingly.

"Be nice," I say as she wedges her bag of popcorn between our bodies. Then I say, "Good crowd tonight."

"*Good crowd tonight,*" Jenna mimics. "We're not here to be social, Molly, so focus! We're here manhunting. Eyes to the front!" she snaps her fingers at me like a dictator and snaps them again, this time in my face, pointing to the ice.

I can't help myself—I roll my eyes at her. Yes, I probably roll my eyes way too much, but I'm telling you, she gets to be a bit much. Despite my irritation at her high-handedness, Jenna doesn't have to tell me twice. We sit like this, attentively watching the action, side by side and not speaking until there are only three minutes left. I've gone from sitting on the fleece blanket to clutching it with white knuckles from the intensity of the game.

My gaze has not left the ice *once*. It is entirely riveted to the center of the hockey rink as if a magnetic force is dragging it there. An asteroid could land behind us and I wouldn't notice.

And damn, did I mention how unbelievably *hot* Weston looks in his uniform?

Normally I'm not really a fan of hockey uniforms because truthfully, those pants make the guys' hips look huge—I mean, I'm talking *wide*—but I will say this: the stark white of River Glen's home jersey sets off Weston's tan skin, currently flushed with sweat and adrenaline, to perfection.

Now, if only those pants were tighter (like, you know, baseball pants) and didn't have all that padding—*that* would be a sight.

Down on the ice, Weston is crouching for more speed, his hockey skates slicing swiftly across the ice. With deft precision, we all watch as he rapidly cuts the puck back and forth with his stick as he rushes the opposing goalie, demonstrating how he earned a reputation as the superstar player he's become.

The goalie flies in front of him and manages to block his attempt. Weston skates wide, and I am at the edge of my seat, holding my breath.

Anyone can see that he has natural talent, and he's definitely on a mission.

Weston passes the puck to Brody Russell, presenting him with a golden opportunity at a chance for a breakaway, but Brody soon loses control of the puck and allows a defender from the opposing team to steal before he can get the puck back to Weston. Everyone in the stands gives a collective groan, and parents are shouting. Our student section is going wild. The puck goes back and forth between RGHS and the opposing team.

Suddenly, Weston gets a centering pass from the corner and blasts it past the goalie's glove. The noise from the crowd is deafening, accompanied by the sirens going off. My ears are ringing. People are jumping in their seats and screaming.

He's done it.

Three goals in one game.

Skating over to his teammates, they quickly celebrate the point, and Weston skates around with his fist in the air. My heart is beating so fast just watching him. *How hot can one guy possibly be?* Then he's skating by, stick in the air as he stares up into the stands, and I receive his message loud and clear.

Those were all for *me*...

***

A few short hours later, it's past eleven o'clock and I'm nestled deep under my down comforter on my back, staring up at the ceiling. It's too dark to see anything but the remnants of small glow-in-the-dark stars sprinkled above my bed from my youth. They're not bright enough to cast a light, but if you strain your eyes, you can still see them casting a dull spark.

I won't lie—as I lie here, a tidal wave of disappointment has washed over me, because I thought *maybe* at this point Weston would have...something. I don't know. I'm embarrassed to even admit it, but I was hoping he would have gotten ahold of me maybe? Texted me? Ugh, what if he lost my number? Which makes me wonder, how did he get my number to begin with? Don't judge me. I know this is ridiculous—after all, we're nothing to each other but noodle buddies—but...you know how girls are, always overthinking things, wishing on stars and praying (when I don't even pray for good grades).

Dear Lord, please let him call me. Please let him like me. Please let me know he just can't stop thinking about me either.

Please, please, please...

As the dark takes over, I make a futile effort to close

my eyes, but all I can do is stare at the ceiling, counting fading stars. I glance over at the alarm clock on my bedside table.

11:11

Make a wish, my head whispers.

I wish Weston would send me a—wait.

Hold on one second.

My phone lights up the dark, indicating I have a new text message.

My stomach flutters, and even though I'm absolutely alone, I reach for it nonchalantly anyway, not wanting to be too eager.

Holy hockey sticks, it's him.

Weston: *You up?*

I swear to you, if I weren't tucked in this bed, I would be doing a happy dance in the middle of my room right now. I resist the urge to pump my fist and scream out in the dark. Instead, I grab a throw pillow and shriek "Ahh!" into it. How horrifying would it be if my parents heard and came running into my room, thinking there was an emergency, or that I was being abducted, giving everyone a heart attack like the one I'm having now? Yeah, exactly. I can see myself explaining it now: *Nothin' to see here, folks! Not being murdered! Just receiving texts from the hottest freaking boy you've never met, in the middle of the night.*

Me: *Yup, wide awake and staring at the ceiling. You?*

Weston: *You made it to the game.*

Well, he certainly doesn't beat around the bush, now does he? How awesome.

I bite my lip, not knowing whether to play coy or just go with it. Either way, I can't believe he's basically calling me out for attending the game simply because he asked me to. How embarrassing. Then again, *he's* admitting that he was watching for me in a *crowd* of people!

Me: *You noticed?*

Weston: *I noticed. My dad noticed. My MOM noticed.*

I begin kicking my legs under the covers in a total freak-out moment, and as my duvet falls on the ground, I rack my brain, wondering what he could possibly mean by that. His mom noticed? Then it dawns on me.

Me: *Lady with the foam finger?*

Weston: *Lol. Yup. She was freaking out when I got home.*

Me: *Why???*

He doesn't respond for what seems like an absolute eternity.

Weston: *For a bunch of reasons.*

Way to leave a girl hanging! I'm totally tempted to ask what reasons, because obviously I am *beyond* dying to know, but he's given me such a vague answer that I don't want to pry, as much as I…want to pry. My fingers hover over the keypad on my phone, and I don't know what to say. First I type, *Oh,* but then I delete it. Then I type, *No biggie,* but I delete that too. Before I can make my brain come up with a cohesive sentence, he responds.

Weston: *Were you impressed?*

Sheesh, what a conceited ass.

But at least it's something I can sink my teeth into.

Me: *Yes, you conceited ass. I was on the edge of my*

seat to the bitter end.

> Weston: *Lol. I aim to please.*

I stare at that sentence, not really knowing what to say, and those flutters are back in my stomach. A million things come to mind, none of them even remotely appropriate for this conversation. Newsflash: I have a tremendously imaginative mind, and by imaginative, I mean vivid…and by vivid, I mean I can out trash-talk my brother.

> Weston: *I noticed you were late. Tsk tsk*
>
> Me: *Shouldn't you have been focused on the game?*
>
> Weston: *And THAT'S the reason my mom was freaking out when I got home.*
>
> Me: *(snort) like you have never been distracted from a game before.*

Again, Weston doesn't respond right away. I sit there in the dark, thinking maybe I went too far. Calling a guy out for creeping on me? *Real smooth, Molly.* Jenna would be having a hysterical fit right now (*not* in a good way) and would probably be hitting me with something at this point too.

After about four minutes of pure torture, my phone finally lights up.

> Weston: *Nope. This would be a first.*

My phone immediately dings again as he sends another text.

> Weston: *I was hoping we could have grabbed something at Kyoto after the game, but my hand had to get wrapped and the trainer took forever.*

Why is he saying these things!

> Me: *Noodles *do* sound good…great. Now I'm hun-*

gry, thanks a lot!

There is yet another long pause before he responds, and I have to question at this point whether he knows *anything at all* about the female species, because if he did, there is no way he would take so long. It's freaking driving me out of my mind, and I have enough energy coursing through my body right now to easily bust out my cross trainers and jog a few miles.

Weston: *So my parents are probably going to freak when they find out I'm asking you this, but...do you have plans this weekend?*

This weekend? As in three short days from now?

Me: *I think I'm free. Why? Did you want to go have those noodles ;)*

Long pause.

I take this time to close my eyes and imagine what his long muscular body looks like stretched out on his bed, in only mesh gym shorts. In my mind, they're red and his chest is bare, defined pecs and strong calf muscles flexing as he decides what he's going to text next.

I bury my face in the pillow and let out a loud groan.

Weston: *No. More like...an actual...idk...date.*

And that's the moment I kick the covers off my bed and let out a blood-curdling scream.

Weston

"Just when you thought you couldn't piss me off even more, you go and outdo yourself." – Brian McGrath to Weston

I have a date.

Holy shit, an actual date.

I haven't had a real one in…well, never.

And my mom is totally going to kill me when she finds out. Correction: my *dad* is totally going to kill me when he finds out. I'm less worried about my mom.

You see, the thing is, even though my parents do pretty well financially, they're still counting on me to receive a hockey scholarship for college. I've been playing since I was little; to say that it consumes my life would be the understatement of the year.

This usually means:

    1. 1. No girlfriend, which means—contrary to popular belief—I tend to not get laid very often, or

not at all, depending on what season it is.

2. 2. No job, which means I have to kiss my dad's ass when I need cash for something.
3. 3. No life.

Most people assume I don't participate in school functions because I'm some kind of insensitive asshole, but that's not the case. The fact is, I don't have the time—never made the time.

If I'm not at hockey practice, I'm sleeping off hockey practice.

Or eating.

As I'm about to slam the door to my locker shut, I grab a Pop-Tart from the dwindling supply on the top shelf. I have one pack left. Fucking Rick is always eating my shit and never replaces any of it. As I rip the silver wrapper open with my teeth—it's cherry, by the way, my favorite—I sling my loaded-down backpack over my shoulder and tug my ball cap down over my eyes in an effort to avoid having to stop and talk to my peers, who loiter in the halls. Unfortunately, I'm forced to raise my head and nod to a few people along my way to the cafeteria.

God am I starving.

I've almost made it as far as the lunchroom when Alexis Peterson flounces up to me and rests her small hand on my upper arm. I let out a loud groan of frustration, but that doesn't stop Alexis from latching on. She's this smallish cheerleader type who appears everywhere she's not wanted. I mean, hasn't she heard of personal space? Even though she's grabbing my arm, she's bouncing in place on the balls of her feet—you know, like *Tigger*, only more annoying.

"Hey, Wes, you have practice after school?" she practically purrs, giving me a toothy grin and twirling a lock of her black hair. I notice that she has lipstick on her teeth and battle the urge to curl my lip in disgust.

"Uh yee-ah, Alexis. Just like every single day of the week..." Now, at this point in our short conversation, she's running her index fingernail up and down my arm, which is bare because I'm wearing a cutoff shirt. *Stupid, stupid, stupid.* I want to swat her hand off me, but instead I just give my arm a quick shake.

It has no effect on her whatsoever. What is it with this chick? Can't she take a hint?

Seriously, man, all I want to do is eat...

The cafeteria just behind her is getting crowded, and the lunch line is growing, but Alexis isn't done with me yet. "So, like, my parents are going to be, like, out of town this weekend..." Her voice trails off meaningfully at the end. I look at the lunch line then impatiently back at Alexis.

What is she freaking talking about?

"Uh yeah," I say mindlessly, staring straight over her head. "That should be fun. You should throw a party." From where I'm standing, I can see Erin Blazer and Derek Hanson taking trays at the beginning of the lunch buffet. They're laughing at something Samantha Granger is saying, and even from here I can see Sam is swatting at them and is *royally* pissed off. Those two are such dicks.

I stifle a laugh.

"Are you even listening to me?" Alexis pouts, pulling on the front of my shirt like a sulky kid begging for attention. I look down to see that her bottom lip is thrust out. Uh, just a little advice ladies: guys don't like girls who act like spoiled brats. The toddler look is a total turnoff.

"Alexis, spit it out, because I'm hungry as *shit* and Blazer's getting all the bread."

"I was actually thinking you could maybe, like, come over and we could like, do stuff."

Like, do stuff?

"Uh, gee, Alexis, I have a date, so…I'll be doing *stuff*…just…not with you." I am able to shrug off her wandering fingers, so I hike my backpack up onto my shoulder and push the hair out of my eyes from under my ball cap. Alexis just stands there, blankly staring at me as if I've sprouted three heads, and I can't help but look at her curiously. "Are you okay?" I ask. Just so we're clear, I don't really give a shit if she's okay; I'm just asking to be polite.

I wave a hand in front of her face to check for vitals.

She finally blinks. Satisfied, I shrug and turn to walk away. I am mere seconds away from being sated by as much government-regulation pizza and crinkle-cut fries that I can eat when I hear a terrible noise.

I guess being a guy, I'm not particularly observant, especially when I'm as hungry as I am. If I were even a tiny bit observant, I would have seen Alexis stiffen and her small fists clench at her sides, and I *definitely* would have been prepared for what came next.

"You *what!*" Alexis screeches from somewhere behind me.

She sounds like a banshee.

Dude, there is no way in hell I'm turning around, even though everyone within fifty yards turns to gawk. That chick is obviously batshit crazy, and clearly there's a reason I had the good sense not to hook up with her. Instead,

I book it to my regular lunch table and dump my backpack before making a beeline for the food.

***

"What the hell was up with Alexis Peterson?" someone asks me a few minutes later as I'm dunking five fries into the sea of ketchup at the edge of my tray at once.

I stuff my mouth. "Batshit crazy," I mumble somewhat audibly.

"Well, I'd still bang her," Erik Gunderson practically shouts, and a chorus of raucous laughter erupts.

"Gunderson, you'd bang your own sister for a slice of pie," Rick hollers in his loud-ass voice. Out of the corner of my eye, I can see the cafeteria attendant take notice of us and change direction, heading right for our table.

"Dude, shut the fuck up. Keep your voice down," I hiss. I swear, my friends are freaking idiots, and I, unfortunately, am their leader.

"What the hell was Alexis blabbering about, anyway? I saw Kristy Rose haul her off into the bathroom." This observation is from Rick. He's sitting across from me, eyeing the last slice of pizza on my plate.

I cover it with my free hand.

"I don't know, man. I wasn't listening to a thing she was saying. Something about me going to her house this weekend and messing around, I guess." As I'm saying this, I arrange the last of my fries on my pizza, fold it in half like a sandwich, dip it in ketchup, and bite down.

"*That* is fucking disgusting," Rick says.

I shrug, chewing. "It all ends up in the same place anyway."

Rick leans his arm over across the table, and his index finger lingers near the corner of my mouth. "Dude, you have a little ketchup right…here…"

I slap his arm away. "Get the fuck away from me, you idiot." I am annoyed, but I also laugh, because sometimes he can be funny, even if he is a complete and total dick.

From where I'm sitting, I have a clear view of the entire area. On the opposite side of the cafeteria is a long bank of windows where someone has painted an advertisement for the upcoming football game and Fall Formal dance, and if you want my opinion, whoever painted it did a shitty job—as in, my half-blind cousin Stuart could have done a better job with it if *both* his eyes were bad.

Oh, and by the way—in case you're at all interested—this year's homecoming is against the Clarksville Panthers and…I'm *pretty* sure we'll get our asses kicked, since all their "real" athletes play hockey.

There are also vending machines in the cafeteria, located right in the corner of the room, which just happens to be the place where Molly Wakefield eats her lunch, as I've recently discovered.

Yeah, discovering that little tidbit was exciting for me too.

I crack open a carton of cold chocolate milk and zero in on my target while I chug it.

Today, she's had her back to me the whole time, but I watch her just the same from under the rim of my cap like I did in the library the other day. I lean back and stretch, flexing my back as Molly's friend gestures wildly beside her. Her friend's brightly colored T-shirt looks splattered with paint, and her long silver earrings catch the sun from outside with every shake of her head.

I rack my brain for the friend's name. Jane. No, wait. Jennifer. Janna? *Whatever.* It happens to be the same blonde chick who has a small seizure every time I walk by.

No lie.

Someone steps in the way and blocks my view, so I have to crane my neck a little to the left. The voices beside me are gradually getting louder as they reenter my stream of consciousness.

"….no freaking way…"

"…Wes…date this weekend…"

"…she is so full of shit… Tell him you don't have a date, McGrath…"

"McGrath? Are you listening?"

Someone hits my arm. "Huh? What?"

Rick and Derek exchange looks, then Derek, who is also sitting across from me, swivels in his seat to survey the room. He even shields his eyes with his palm, like he's saluting the sea of students. What a wise-ass. "Okay, so who were you just checking out?"

"No one." The lie rolls off my tongue, and I crack open another carton of milk and guzzle it down, crushing the carton on the table with my palm when I'm done. No way in hell am I going to tell these douchebags I have a date with Molly Wakefield, the one highlight of my dismally social-life-free senior year. I would never hear the end of it.

"Bullshit, dude. You spaced out."

"That's because nothing you say interests me. In fact, I'm done here." I grab the edge of my tray before collecting my backpack and rising from my seat at the same time Molly stands at her table across the room.

I stand unmoving and watch her instead of walking away.

She's facing me, and our eyes connect. Finally, Molly gives me a small self-conscious wave, and if the Three Assholes of the Apocalypse weren't sitting in front of me, I'd probably wave back. Her long hair is in a braid that's cascading over her shoulder, and she's wearing a cute pink dress.

Man, she's pretty.

My lips curl slightly into a small smile.

"*Are you fucking kidding me, Weston?* Molly Wakefield?" Rick picks up his tray and then instantly slams it back onto the table in a rage, sending a few fries scattering across its surface. "You asshole."

His pronouncement doesn't surprise me, and quite honestly, I don't give a crap if he's upset. You're probably wondering if there's such a thing as "guy code". The answer is yes, but in my opinion, it doesn't apply in this case. Why? Well, for starters:

1. Rick is my teammate, but he is not my friend. He's thrown me under the bus so many times I've lost count.
2. He once tried to sleep with my cousin, Tracy.
3. Lastly—oh, that's right. I don't give a shit about his feelings.

I blow out a puff of air so I don't lose my temper, but I can already feel my nostrils flaring, a telltale sign that I'm about to. As calmly as I can, I set my backpack and tray down, rest my palms against the edge of the table, and lean over so that my face is inches from Rick's. The brim of my hat almost touches his forehead.

I am aware of hundreds of watchful eyes boring into me.

"Is there a problem?" This voice does not sound like my own; this voice is low and menacing.

"Yeah, *you're* my goddamn problem." Rick's eyes dart over to where the lunch attendant is standing, and he stays embedded in his seat, but he's clearly itching for a fight.

"Why is that?" I probe.

"You *know* I asked her out," he says through gritted teeth, drawing his sentence out slowly. "You were standing right there."

I frown at him through narrowed eyes, leaning closer. "And what was her answer?"

Rick shrugs coolly, but his demeanor is anything but. "She'll come around."

I laugh right then, and I have to admit, even to my own ears it sounds slightly maniacal.

"Yeah? Well *you* scare the *shit* out of her." I quietly snarl, suddenly realizing it as the awful truth. That day in the hallway when Rick was harassing Molly for a date, I should have shoved his punk ass up against my locker. She looked so scared. Shit, the more I remember it, the more pissed off I become. "Do yourself a favor, *Rick*," I spit out sarcastically. "Don't talk to her. Don't talk *about* her. Hell, don't even *look* at her. Because if you do, I will find out, and then I will beat the *shit* out of you." My triceps flex and my shoulders are drawn taut. "Do we have an understanding?"

Faintly, I hear Erik Gunderson in the background say,

"Dayyuumm."

I stay rooted to the spot, waiting on his answer. We're both breathing heavily, and I know from past experience what Rick looks like when he wants to punch someone in the face. It's the same look he's giving me now.

"Why do you even care?" he finally asks with a snort. "If you're trying to get in her pants, you're wasting your time. That chick ain't givin' it up for *nobody*." He looks around for support, trying to make our friends laugh but failing miserably.

"I'm sorry, but it seems like you're not hearing me. Stay. Away. From. Molly."

Finally, he gives a barely imperceptible nod.

I collect my stuff and strut away, conceited ass that I am.

***

"Mom, I have to talk to you about something," I mumble gruffly as I pull out the barstool at the kitchen counter. My mom is standing at the stove with her back to me, stirring what smells like vegetable stir-fry. She taps the wooden spoon on the pan and turns to face me, laying the spoon down. Wiping her hands on a towel, she comes over and leans her elbows on the counter.

"This sounds serious. Is everything okay?"

Let's see, how do I put this...

"Oh man. I don't even know how to say this." I run my fingers through my shaggy hair as my mom leans over and grabs my forearm.

"Sweetheart, now you're scaring me. What is it? Tell Mom."

"I don't want you to be pissed at me."

"Weston Richard McGrath, you tell me right now what is wrong or you're going to be in a shit storm of trouble, young man."

I let out the long breath I've been holding and count to three before I say, "I have a date this weekend. I…I asked someone on a date."

My mom stares at me slack-jawed.

Ah shit, I've rendered her speechless.

Molly

11

"Better to arrive late than to arrive ugly!" – Darcy Gilmore, blogger

The rest of the week has crawled by at a snail's pace, and thank God it's finally Saturday night. Unfortunately, I'm freaking out. Today was the worst. I literally could not focus the entire day because of the text I received first thing when I woke up.

Weston: *I have practice but will text you after*

And he did. All morning I waited for that promised text, shuffling around the house. I carried my phone around in the palm of my hand like it was my job, and when Weston's text finally came, unfortunately, I was sitting next to my mom on the couch.

Talk about embarrassing. You know moms want to talk about everything once they get a whiff of gossip, and I ended up having to tell her every tiny detail leading up to this point.

Oh Lord, I could throw up right now. I have managed to toss almost every article of clothing from my closet onto my floor in a fit of *so many clothes and nothing to wear*.

Where is Jenna? She's supposed to be here helping me! It's five o'clock. Weston will be here in an hour. I race to the window and throw back the curtains. Great. Her car is in the driveway. Opening my bedroom door, I holler, "Jenna, get your butt up here! I need you!"

"Okay, pretty girl, calm down." Jenna laughs as she trots down the hallway toward my room. She's got on bright green pants and a gray sweatshirt, and I notice she's dipped the ends of her long blonde locks in pink Kool-Aid. When the heck did she do that? I just saw her last night…

She stops in the threshold of my room, eyeing the clothes that have been strewn everywhere, and her eyes get real wide. "What the…?"

I stand there helplessly, arms spread in desperation. "Help," I squeak out.

"Oh my god, Molls, you have to get a grip. Let's start by putting this all away so I can at least see what you have to work with. *Ugh*, girl, you are crazy." Yeah, you heard right; the girl wearing neon pants is calling *me* crazy. She bends at the waist and starts picking up clothes, placing them back on the hangers that have been haphazardly thrown on the ground. "Hmm," she mumbles in thought. "This is kind of cute." She lays a striped navy tank top on my bed.

"Jenna, its cold out!" I whimper.

"Do you want my help or not?"

"Yes."

"Then start helping me clean up this mess you made. Sheesh. What am I, your mother?"

"I'm sorry. I'm just so nervous." I start biting my thumbnail, and almost immediately, Jenna slaps the hand out of my mouth and grabs me by the shoulders. She gives me a firm shake.

"You look at me. *Look!*" She points at her eyes with two fingers. "Molly, you're funny and gorgeous. That great hunk of a hockey star is *lucky* to be going out with you tonight. Now get it together before I slap you."

"Do I have to wear something so tight?" I start whining again as my best friend cleans my room.

"No, but you have to give him a little peek at the goods. Come on, get real—he's a guy, and you have a great rack."

"But what if we end up go-carting or something?"

Jenna turns and levels me with a stare. Okay, never mind. "Wear a turtleneck on your own time, okay, Gidget?" Newsflash, for those of you not familiar: Gidget was a television character in the sixties and she was kind of a giant nerd. "Here. We'll do these for sure." Jenna pulls out a pair of dark stretch skinny jeans. "If you're lucky, he'll slap your ass a few times."

I open my mouth to respond, but nothing comes out.

It doesn't take her long to pick out an entire ensemble, complete with shoes, a shirt, and jewelry. Motioning to the vanity, she pats my desk chair. "Come on, let's get your hair and makeup done." With the determined expression on her face, she could pass for an Army drill sergeant.

Thank god for best friends.

Weston

I've been driving in the country for a few miles when I finally come to a really long driveway. From the road, I can make out a large stone house with a wraparound porch and a high-peaked roof. The mailbox is on the opposite side of the street, and it's getting dark out already, so I roll down my window to double check the house number: 932.

I let out a nervous breath.

Yup, this is definitely it.

I turn in. The whole driveway is blacktop, and there are lampposts lining the road about every seventy-five feet. It's only early October, but someone has already tied corn stalks to the black columns in preparation for fall, and a few of them have large pumpkins sitting next to them on the ground. I pull up to the turnaround and sit facing a large red vinyl Wisconsin Badgers flag that's flapping in the breeze off the basketball pole next to the garage. Next to that hangs another red flag with a large number 19 on it.

I reach forward and turn the volume down on the radio then cut my engine. I give my legs and back a good stretch before I open the door, then stretch again once my feet hit the ground.

The walk up to Molly's front door isn't long, but by the time I reach it, my palms are good and sweaty. I feel like I've just skated a few practice laps in the heat. Why am I so damn nervous? My hands are fidgety, so I shove them inside my pockets.

Then I take them out.

Crap. What do I do while I'm standing here? I bounce

a few times on the balls of my feet and loosen my shoulders like I'm preparing for a mixed martial arts fight. Then I stop, because shit, if someone's watching from a window, they probably think I look like a complete jackass out here.

I wipe my hands on my jeans and raise my fist to knock.

Almost immediately, a dog starts barking wildly inside the house, and I can hear someone shouting for it to 'go lay down.'

The door opens.

A woman who is so obviously Molly's mom looks back at me with a pleasant smile on her face, and wow does she look like her daughter. She is on the taller side and slender, with the same brownish red hair as Molly's. She even has freckles on the bridge of her nose, too. She's very pretty—not as pretty as Molly, obviously, but still…I would put her at MILF status for sure.

"Weston, I presume?" she asks casually. That small smile still pinned to her lips, Mrs. Wakefield assesses me, her eyes taking me in from head to toe until I can feel her staring holes into my tattoo-covered arm. I resist the instinct to cross my arms. Still, her face remains impassive, and if the sight of my tats offends her, she's hiding it well.

Cool.

"Yes ma'am, pleased to meet you." I stick my hand out for her to shake, which she does, and I pray to God it isn't clammy. Damn, maybe I should have wiped them on my jeans again. "Is Molly home?"

Her mom chuckles softly, giving me another onceover and shaking her head from side to side as if she can't believe I'm standing in her foyer. "As if she'd miss this. Come on in." She motions me in with her hand, and the door widens as she steps aside to let me in.

"Thanks." I don't know what else to say. "Those UW flags outside are great."

"Ah, yes, the flags. Mr. Wakefield had those made when Matthew, our son, signed his letter of intent to play for Madison a few years ago, but let's not talk about him. I hear you're a player yourself."

Player myself...? Oh! She means I'm a *hockey player,* not that I play girls. "Yes ma'am. I'm a forward."

"We haven't been to any of the games at the high school lately, but we hear you're very good. Maybe we'll have to come cheer you on. Mr. Wakefield loves hockey, as you've probably guessed."

"Yes ma'am." Shit, I sound like a *freaking idiot.* "Sorry I keep repeating myself. I don't do this very often." Mrs. Wakefield cocks her head and smiles like she's talking to a child.

"Don't tell me you're nervous?"

"You have no idea."

"Well, I won't torture you any longer. I'll go let Molly know you're here, even though I'm sure she's listening from upstairs." She pats me on the arm.

"Thank you, Mrs. Wakefield," I say as she starts walking up the beige carpeted stairs. Then, as if she just can't help herself, she turns back and glances at me standing in her foyer. I swear she mumbles, *Holy crap, Molly,* but it's either my ego messing with my head or a case of nerves.

Upstairs, some faint chatter is soon followed by footsteps padding down the hallway, and my senses go on alert as Molly rounds the corner.

Barefoot, she is dangling a pair of shoes by her index finger.

I blink.

Coming down the stairs, Molly looks incredible in her tight-ass skinny jeans. They're dark, ending mid-calf, and damn if even her ankles are sexy. She shoots me a shy smile and flips her long wavy hair. Her fitted top is white and strapless, setting off her golden skin and flaring out at the bottom. Around her waist is a thin belt. Molly's smooth shoulders and arms are completely bare, and I try hard—I really do—but I can't stop myself from checking out her cleavage.

Naturally I wonder if she's wearing a bra, because from where I'm standing, it looks like she's not, and holy hell does she have great boobs. Why have I never noticed before?

Someone clears their throat, and I glance up to see Mrs. Wakefield staring holes into me with her arms crossed.

Shit.

Molly

Okay, don't think for one second I don't see Weston checking out my chest, which I will admit is displayed quite nicely, compliments of my new strapless peplum top. As I make my way toward him, I feel like I've entered a parallel universe. I cannot believe I have a date with this boy.

This hottie. This un-gettable get.

Can I call him a stud muffin? I know, I know—lame, right?

Weston is standing at the bottom of the stairs with this hooded expression on his face that looks something like… lust. His scrutiny is the one thing making my stomach flutter—well, that and the fact that it looks like he wants to tackle me to the ground.

Oh God, I'm in way over my head. I think I might throw up.

Suddenly, my mom's loud throat-clearing fit interrupts any nervous nausea I'm feeling—and yeah, I know I'm totally going to get in trouble for it later, but I send her a hard look over my shoulder that says, *For the love of God, please go away.*

Weston stands there awkwardly and shoves those masculine hands of his into the pockets of his jeans. His appearance has actually shocked me; not only is he wearing a pressed polo shirt and dress pants, but—

"You cut your hair," is the first thing I say to him, a little breathlessly. Before I can stop myself—and because, let's be honest, I *want* to—I walk over and brush the newly shorn strands above his ears through my fingers. He shivers. "Why?" I whisper as I pull my hand away. In response, his dark brown eyes study my face. So quickly I almost miss it, they dart back down between the valley of my breasts before settling on my lips, then my eyes.

"It seemed…like the right time to get a haircut?"

His voice makes my girly bits tingle and he smells incredible.

I wrinkle my brows. The 'right time' to get a haircut… Okay, what the heck is that supposed to mean? When will I ever understand guys?

"Whew! Okay then! You kids should be on your way,"

my mom practically shouts, looking back and forth between us. "Young man, please remember your manners tonight and act like a gentleman. Oh, and Molly, your brother texted me while you were getting dressed. He's coming home tonight."

Say *what*!

Shit, shit, double shit. I contort my face in confusion, which I will admit is *not* a good look for me. "He is? That makes zero sense. He has a game tomorrow." I sneak a peek at Weston, and his face has actually lit up like a Christmas tree.

God is he hot—ugh, especially with that short hair.

I want to touch it again. Is that so wrong?

"Well, I kind of let the cat out of the bag about you having a date tonight…" she says slowly with her hands spread wide as if to say, *Hey, what do you expect?* I can tell she doesn't want me to be embarrassed, but whoops! Too late!

I throw my hands up, groaning. "You 'kind of' told him I had a date? Great. Just great."

"Is that a bad thing?" Weston asks. In his mind, he's probably thinking, *Sweet, this is great news!* Imagine getting to meet *the* Matthew Wakefield, local hero finishing out his collegiate career at a Big Ten school and recently becoming the third overall pick in the NHL draft, to the Anaheim Ducks. Matthew was the fifth American selected in the first round—normally its lots of Canadians or Russians who go first.

He is a local legend.

I mean, kids from our hometown rarely go on to play professional sports. To say that I am dreading—yes, dreading—having to introduce my egotistical brother to my date would be a gross understatement.

Matthew is a total asshat.

"Let's see, how do I put this…?" I arch my fingers into a steeple and look up at the ceiling. "He *will* be waiting for us when we get back. Well, actually, no, I shouldn't say *us*…I should say you. Matthew will be waiting for *you*. "

My mom giggles nervously.

"*Sweet.*"

Like I said—I will never understand guys.

12

Weston

"I'm not always sarcastic. Sometimes I'm asleep." – Weston

If you're thinking I got my hair cut because I'm going on this date, you'd be correct. Actually, as soon as I told my mom I had a date, she kind of had a mini-spaz attack and immediately insisted I get "cleaned up for that nice-looking girl from the hockey game." Of course, this was all done after lecturing me on prioritizing my life and activities, which go something like this:

1. Family, followed very closely by
2. School—got to always be thinking of that scholarship—then of course
3. Hockey.

And coming in a very far distant last place after about thirty things in front of it: girls.

Speaking of girls…I get an eyeful of Molly's backside

as she hoists herself up into my shiny black truck before I shut the door behind her; I am a gentleman, after all. Jogging around to the driver's side, I hop up into the cab myself and immediately begin strapping on my seatbelt. Safety first, people, safety first.

"Whose…?" Molly is looking around the inside of my dad's Hummer with a furrow to her brow.

"My dad's. Is this okay? I didn't want to make it awkward by showing up on my bike. I don't want your parents to have any objections." I look over and can't help but think she looks great sitting beside me.

When did all this happen? Since when do I lie awake at night thinking about the same girl and watching for her in the halls at school? And when did I get so mushy? Changing my ride, holding doors open, getting my hair cut? Am I out of my damn mind? Romance is for saps and pussies, and I'm neither.

"That was very thoughtful, thank you. It would have sucked if they made me stay home," Molly says, relaxing her elbow on the center console. Her body is naturally leaning toward me and is just close enough to catch a whiff of her…not perfume, something else. Subtly, I inhale the smell of citrus…or maybe it's strawberries.

Her shoulders are bare, and she has a jacket or shawl or whatever wadded up on her lap. It would be so easy to lean in just a little farther and plant one on her glossy pink lips. The corners of her mouth are pulled into a nervous smile, and what I wouldn't give to suck on that pouty lower lip.

Instead, I turn the key and start the ignition, shifting uncomfortably in my seat.

Molly

"So, where are we headed?" I ask, trying to come off as nonchalant. I was going to say, *Where are you taking me?* but that just makes me think *take me*, which makes me think of sex and making out, and who can concentrate with those thoughts on the brain?

Not me.

"You ate, right?" He glances over with his dark eyebrows raised, his hands clutching the steering wheel.

"Yes, just like you instructed me to," I say, teasing him with a smile on my face. He was very clear in his text: *Make sure you eat b4 I pick u up.*

"Good, because there's no human food where we're going." A wry smile crosses his lips, sending a shiver through my body. I take a deep breath and look out the window at the landscape going by to distract myself. Soon, Weston gets on the interstate and we're headed east.

"Are we going into the city?"

"Stop asking questions and being so nosey."

I let out an exaggerated huff and fidget with the black jacket in my lap. I've been instructed by Jenna *not* to wear it; it's for emergency cold temperatures *only*. And I quote: *"You listen and you listen good, Molly Wakefield."* She points at me like she's a trial lawyer and I'm on the witness stand. *"I busted my ass getting you ready for the date of our life—I mean* your *life. Do not ruin this outfit by wearing a jacket. This jacket is for emergency. Use. Only."* She grips the jacket, shaking it at me in her clutched hand with every enunciated word. *"How do you expect Weston to lust after you if you cover up your girl bits? Now, I'm going to slowly hand it over, but not willingly..."*

Of course, that lecture only led me to believe Jenna *might* be a tad bit unstable.

"Sorry, I can't help it. I have an active imagination. I'm sitting over here in my little corner, hoping you're not taking me out of town to murder me."

Weston laughs, the glorious sound filling the cab of the truck. "Trust me on this: I'd rather be doing *other* things to you." The comment rolls off his tongue airily. "Oh shit, did I say that out loud?"

I'm silent for a few heartbeats, my mind racking for something to say. Finally I shrug and say, "Well, I guess that's good to know."

We both laugh.

"Molly, that was possibly the coolest way any chick could have responded."

I throw my hands up. "Don't get me wrong, I'm not saying it wasn't *pervy*, but I'm willing to overlook it. I mean, you did get your hair cut for me and all." I tease him and he actually blushes. Even in the dim light I can see the color rising on his neck.

He looks more like a boy than the cocky guy who struts around school like he owns it.

A loud chirping sound fills the cab of the truck, and we both realize Weston's phone is ringing. Like a gentleman, he ignores it, and for some reason this pleases me. He seems like the kind of guy who wouldn't think twice about taking a phone call while he's on a date, 'cause normally, it just seems like he doesn't...give a shit.

"Don't you at least want to see who that was?" I ask,

smiling.

"No. The only person I want to talk to is sitting right next to me." He smiles over at me and his face transforms. His teeth are bright white against his freshly shaved skin. His eyebrows are dark and frame his eyes, making me want to slide over and kiss his face all over.

Oh crap.

Newsflash: guys can't just go around saying romantic shit like that! *The only person I want to talk to is sitting right next to me*—now what the hell am I supposed to say? Don't you think that's a tad too upfront for our age—too honest? I glance out the window, trying to conjure up some semblance of an intelligent response. *Someone help me!* Where is Jenna when I need her?

On second thought, her advice would probably be terrible, and probably…slutty.

Which…at this juncture, doesn't seem like such a bad idea after all.

If I'm being honest.

Heat rises in my face, and I look back at Weston, who has his eyes on the road.

Good boy.

I slowly let my eyes graze his body, starting with the hard thighs in the dark dress pants he's wearing. Even though I can't actually see them, I know the abs under that bright aqua polo shirt are flat, flat and chiseled—at least in my vivid imagination they are. *Flat, chiseled, and sweaty…* I swallow hard and bite my lower lip. He has both hands clutching the wheel, and I study his tattoos. Now I'm just checking out his arms. The muscles in his forearms flex, and when he turns his head toward me, our eyes meet.

I smile shyly, embarrassed to be caught checking him out.

Weston clears his throat loudly, and with a slight adolescent squeak, he manages, "So, uh…did you have fun at the game this week?"

Oh, thank god he's asking questions. I thought this was going to be awkward.

"Honestly, it was so intense. I was practically chewing on my blanket."

"Really?" He seems surprised, although I'm not sure why.

"Are you kidding me? When Cole Murdock scored on that trick shot during the third quarter by coming straight up the middle, I almost *wet* myself." I can't keep the enthusiasm out of my voice, and *of course I would say something like that out loud.*

Weston makes a *pfft* sound and scoffs, trying not to sound impressed by my jargon, but lips don't lie—he is all smiles. "Please, that was such a rookie move. Anyone could have pulled that off. Besides, Murdock is a puss—uhh…" His voice trails off.

"I'm sorry, what were you about to call him? Cole Murdock is a *what*…?" I cup my hand around my ear and lean in like I'm hard of hearing. Chuckling, I flop back against the seat again and fold my arms across my chest, smirking with satisfaction. "Nice one, Weston." He looks at me, and his eyes flicker to my boobs, which are currently being plumped up further by my arms. He's totally getting an eyeful.

Whoops.

"You can call me Wes, you know."

Hmmm. "What if I don't want to?" I ask boldly with a slightly flirty lilt to my voice. *Great, next I'll be twirling my hair around my finger and giggling at him.* "I like the name Weston. It suits you."

"Honestly, you can call me anything you want."

"Aww, I bet you say that to all the girls." *Flirt, flirt, flirt,* my subconscious shouts at me.

This earns me a queer look, and he tips his head sideways as he looks out the front windshield at the road ahead of him. "Um, yeah…no. There are no other girls. Nice try though."

Weston

It's really hard to concentrate on driving with Molly sitting there flirting, looking ten kinds of sexy. Her tan boobs are pushed up in that white strapless top, and this fantasy of pulling over onto the side of the road and trailing wet kisses up and down her neck is seriously fucking with my head. I can barely keep my eyes on the road, so I clutch the steering wheel tighter. She seriously needs to stop talking, because everything coming out of her pert little mouth is rendering me practically senseless.

I can barely form an intelligible sentence.

What the fuck?

Molly and I continue to talk easily, but my responses… er, I can't tell you what is coming out of my mouth at this moment—mostly grunting and lots of "Uh huh, yeah," because I can't focus on the conversation. My sole goal is to get us to our destination in one piece.

As I sit there, once again my mind wanders to the fact that Molly isn't dating anyone. Why is she single? Jeez, I've never met anyone so funny, smart, and cute. Trust me when I say this: a lot of girls cross my path on a regular basis—girls who want to be with me because I'm an athlete, and not much else. They know I'm headed to a Division One school, probably the pros after that, and they want to say they've screwed me. It wouldn't matter if I wasn't good-looking. Take Rick for example. In my opinion, his face is fucked up, and that dude can still get a blow job any time of the day.

There's just something about Molly.

Something…different.

Like, she's got class. Plus, as an added bonus, Molly knows more shit about hockey than most guys who sit at my lunch table. Talk about a complete turn-on. I almost came in my pants when she said *trick shot*.

Her voice breaks into my thoughts as I turn into a parking lot, and I realize I've been daydreaming far too long.

"The aquarium? Weston, this is…*incredible!*" She's got this doe-eyed expression across her face as I pull into the aquarium's parking structure. I roll down my window as I pull up to the automated teller, push the large round green button for a ticket stub, and once I have it, I slap it on my dash.

Soon we're approaching the building, and I bust ahead so I can hold the door for her. She's got her jacket on, and damn if I don't mourn the loss of the view of her bare shoulders.

13

Molly

"You want my advice? Because I'm gonna give it to you, anyway. If you want this guy, you just have to kiss the shit out of the dumb bastard." – Jenna

We're walking past the moon jellyfish exhibition when Weston suggests we stop and sit on the bench seated in front of the wall-size aquarium. The room where the exhibit is housed is actually dark, and the tank in front of us is dark too. Only the soft blue glow from the jellyfish lights up the room.

There is an unoccupied bench directly in front of the huge reservoir of sea life, so that's where we sit. Pulsing and drifting in a weightless dance, the jellyfish look like ghosts with their translucent bodies lit by a black light. Soft music is being pumped into the room, and I have to admit, this has been the perfect date.

I am aware of Weston's soft breathing beside me and the heat from his large body. Our thighs and hips are touching, and every cell in my body is humming from the contact.

We sit for several minutes without speaking, content to watch hundreds of glowing sea creatures dance a water ballet in front of us. The sight is breathtaking.

"What are you thinking about right now?" Weston's voice breaks the silence, and it's so random I throw my head back and laugh. The sound echoes off the walls in the hollow cavernous room, and I have to admit that, even to my own ears, it sounds throaty and kind of…erotic.

"I thought guys *hated* that question. That's right up there with *Do these jeans make me look fat?*"

"Yeah, I guess I never got that memo. Maybe I shouldn't have asked." Then he gives me a sideways glance. "So…"

"Oh okay. You want me to play along, I see. What am I thinking about, what am I thinking about…" I tap on my chin, pretending to ponder my answer. "Well, I was thinking about how the jellyfish look like floating ballerinas." I laugh again at his scrunched-up expression. "Does that satisfy your curiosity?"

"Well, no, actually. That answer *sucked*."

"Did it leave you unfulfilled?" I tease.

"Uh, *yeah,* it did."

My mom and I always say we're 'unfulfilled' when we spend a whole day shopping and leave the mall without having purchased anything fun. I remember this one time, we spent an *entire* day going to garage sales, and all I spent was six dollars on an old chandelier I spray painted for my bedroom and two bucks on a pair of jeans. Ugh, did I feel empty inside that day. I chuckle at my own fond memory.

We're quiet for a bit in companionable silence, and then I murmur, "It's so peaceful here. Thank you for bringing me." I'm tempted to lay my head on his shoulder but can't dig deep enough to gather up the courage. Instead, our eyes stay glued to the blue glowing jellyfish that pulse and float in front of us, up…then down…up…then down…slow and languishing like a lullaby. Watching them is spellbinding, and I can see how it would be therapeutic.

A person could stay here all day.

Soon, we're back to quietly talking in hushed tones. Maybe it's just us, but the atmosphere just makes you want to whisper. We talk about his sister Kendall, and he tells me about Zoe, the sister he lost to a battle to childhood leukemia almost five years ago at the tender age of seven. Zoe, the one name tattooed on his arm.

We talk about hockey. Soccer. Traveling. I tell him about my job, and am shocked to discover he's never had one because he's never had the time. He reveals his love of the Harry Potter series (mindless books he doesn't have to think too much about while reading), and I blush and stutter through telling him my favorite genre is teen romance.

How embarrassing.

We sit there while the minutes fly by, and a while later, around the corner comes a young couple. Maybe just a few years older than Weston and I, they slowly walk over to the moon jellyfish exhibit and stand directly in front of the tank—directly in front of us, actually. They're both dressed very casually in jeans, but there is chemistry between them that has me guessing they're on a date. Okay, I don't have to guess; it's pretty obvious.

"Really, *that's* where they're going to stand?" Weston deadpans from the side of his mouth, gesturing to the couple with his hand. Because he's almost whispering and there's music filtering through the room, I lean in a little closer to hear what he's saying and catch a whiff of his cologne. My eyes flit to the V of his polo shirt, and I glace at the exposed hollow of his throat.

Drool.

"No kidding! What's *that* all about?" I complain. "There's a whole room full of these things. Go over there." I point to a spot farther down.

He lets out a sigh. "Well, I suppose we *could* head out. We have been here for over two hours…"

"Plus, there *is* that forty-five-minute drive home…." I point out, trying to be helpful.

Weston thinks for a few seconds, and then says, "*Or*… we could stop for ice cream?"

"Yes!" Oh shit, did that sound too eager or desperate? "Fantastic idea."

Best. Idea. Ever.

I knew there was a reason I liked him.

Weston

"What are you getting?"

I look down into the freezer of ice cream then back up at the menu board hanging on the back wall behind the counter of the ice cream shop. It's a fifties-themed diner with a soda fountain, and the kid behind the counter is wearing a white smock, candy-cane striped shirt, and a disposable paper hat. Based on the nametag pinned to his smock, his name is Scott, and now I feel bad for him because he looks like a fucking douchebag. He's probably what, seventeen? We actually drove almost all the way back to River Glen before stopping so we wouldn't have such a hike after our treat, and technically we're just in the next town over, so now we can take our time.

"I think I know what I want, but ladies first." I plant my elbow on the counter and lean back on it so I'm granted a frontal view as Molly stares up at the menu board, biting her lower lip.

Nonchalantly—at least I think so, anyway—I look her up and down. She's got on these high shoes that tie around her slender ankles, and the toes peeking through are painted a bright shade of pink. I was never one for feet, but hers are pretty damn sexy.

"Hmmm…" She hums with indecision. "I'll…have…" Her head tips to the side, and it's so endearing I can't help but smile. She catches me and chides, "Stop doing that."

"Doing what?"

"Stop distracting me." She swipes at me with the back of her hand but misses, eyes still staring up at the menu board, teeth still biting her lip.

"How am *I* distracting *you*?" Seriously, all damn night she's been driving me crazy—in the best possible way, of course.

Molly levels me with those bright green eyes but finds it hard to keep a straight face. She reaches for my forearm and pulls me to a standing position, releasing my arm quickly like she's been burned. It's the first time we've touched—ever—and holy shit, I can still feel the imprint from her fingers lingering on my skin. "Here, since you know what you want, why don't you go first."

Scott, the kid behind the counter, has his eyes glued on Molly during this whole playful exchange, and I take one step closer to her, marking my territory.

Look away, kid. Look away.

"That one's easy. I'll have a turtle sundae—four scoops of ice cream, extra pecans, extra hot fudge, extra cherries." I slap my palm on the counter for emphasis then shoot my fingers pointedly at Molly like a gun. "And go."

She raises her eyebrows at me, probably impressed that I eat ice cream like such a boss.

"Give me…the flavor of the day, one scoop, in a chocolate waffle cone." She smiles brightly, pleased with herself for finally having made up her mind.

"Boring." I fake a yawn, patting my mouth. Molly bumps me playfully with her shoulder. "Let's go sit at that table while we wait for young Scott here to fix our dessert." I'm not proud to admit it, but I give the kid an arrogant smirk before placing my hand on the small of Molly's back, guiding her to a small corner booth, my palm so low on her backside I'm practically stroking her ass.

Any excuse to touch her, right?

14

Molly

"Make him work real hard for that first kiss…okay, maybe not that *hard." – Jenna, totally contradicting herself*

"Well, I guess this is me." I state the obvious as Weston pulls his dad's Hummer into the turnaround in front of my house and cuts the engine. The porch lights shine their soft glow into the cab, and suddenly the air is hotter and the atmosphere is thick with expectation. There is a strip of light shining across his eyes and the rest of his face is bathed in shadows, as if he's wearing a mask. I look over to the garage, inwardly groaning when I see Matt's white Tahoe parked next to my Wrangler. *Shit, shit, double shit.* The lights are on inside the house, and I know the longer we sit here, the less time we have before Matt comes busting out of the house to interrogate my date.

I draw in a long breath then let it slowly out—a move learned in yoga class—and turn to Weston, who has his arm stretched out with his hand on the back of my headrest. Just the close proximity of that hand—the hand that's not even *doing* anything but *resting* there, for heaven's sake—has my heart fluttering like a butterfly being tossed in the breeze.

Weston glances at the house. "Yeah, I guess this is your stop." His eyes shine and crinkle at the corners, and his lips lift into a smile, the kind of smile that makes me want to lean over and kiss the crook of his lips.

I glance down at the large center console positioned between us and frown. *Crap,* that's inconvenient. Now I can't get any closer by scooting over. "Walk me to the door?"

Weston

I jog around to Molly's side of the car to get her door, the whole time wondering if she's the type of girl who kisses on the first date. *God, I hope so.* We walk leisurely up the porch steps, taking them slowly one at a time, neither of us in a hurry to reach the top.

The black jacket Molly had been wearing earlier on the date has since been removed, and her shoulders are smooth and shimmery. "Do you have something on your arms? It looks like…glitter?" I ask.

"Yeah, it's, uh, body dust. Jenna practically had to hold me down to get it on me." She scoffs with a laugh, running her hands up and down her arms self-consciously. "It's not normally my thing."

"I'm not *complaining*."

"It's edible," she abruptly blurts out, then looks horrified, but I suddenly find this the most fascinating thing she's said all night. Wow, how did I not know this before? Girls have body stuff that you can eat? That's totally weird, and also *hot*. "I'm sorry, I don't know why I said that."

"Um, I hate to break it to you, Molly, but edible body glitter just became my new favorite thing as of *right* this second."

"Well…then I guess it's my new favorite thing too."

"So I'm wondering…do you think we should just kiss already to break this tension?" I suggest with a good deal of hope in my voice, extending my right hand toward her. Smiling, Molly takes it and steps toward me as I tug, pulling her against me.

Molly

With our bodies pressed this close together, it's hard not to notice every solid muscle of Weston's firm body. Resting both my hands on his firm chest, I let them roam a little before snaking them unhurriedly around to his back.

I've never in my life felt a guy up before, but he must like it, because it's earning me a low growl of approval before Weston tips his head down and presses his lips lightly to my forehead. He trails them down to my temple, kissing the delicate skin by my eyes. I let out a long, satisfied sigh as he pushes my hair back with his large hand, the contact with my bare skin sending a ripple of electricity down my spine. Weston leans back to look in my eyes then, grinning, continues lavishing kisses near my ear, nipping at my lobe with his teeth.

My eyes flutter closed as his tongue licks the side of my neck, his mouth searing my collarbone. He lets out an "Mmmm" and in my drunk-like stupor, I vow to thank Jenna later for the vanilla-flavored body dust.

She would absolutely kill me right now for not playing hard to get—*make him work for it then leave him wanting it*, she told me no less than ten times. Also, it's hard to forget you're standing on your parents' front porch with lights shining on you, but with Weston's hot breath on my body, making me insane for more, I can't even remember what *state* we live in.

Weston is inhaling the scent of my almond shampoo while running his fingertips up and down my back, settling them on my sides and flexing his fingers before pressing them into my hips. "You're so beautiful," he whispers.

I know he's trying to control himself, but all of his feather-light touching makes me want to drag him into the bushes like a caveman and rip off his clothes.

I'm ten seconds from actually doing it, too.

Tipping my head to give him better access to my neck, our breathing becomes labored as his warm lips trail kisses down the side of my neck. I can't take it anymore. I have waited too long to feel his lips pressed against mine, and I'm not waiting a second longer. "Kiss me," I demand almost incoherently under the porch light, tipping my chin up so he can easily find my mouth.

"God, you're so fucking hot," he groans out just before his lips touch mine. His tongue flicks the corner of my mouth before sucking on my bottom lip. I immediately open my mouth, and he slides his tongue in, no preamble or dancing around it.

Our kiss is scorching hot and wet and sloppy.

He could drool all over me and I wouldn't care.

Heaven.

Bliss.

It's perfect. *He's* perfect.

My hands wander up his broad muscular back, and I trail my index fingers up his spine until I reach the collar of his shirt. Instead of running my fingers through his hair, I tease the back of his neck by lightly drawing circles with my nails.

It must be driving him wild, because Weston's hands both grab my ass and pull me firmly against his crotch.

Every cell in *every* inch of my body is tingling. *I am on fire.* I wouldn't be surprised if my hair was sticking straight up. I am positively vibrating. I can't get enough of him, and I let him know by moaning loudly into his mouth like a wanton trollop. All the values I've ever been taught about acting like a lady fly out the window as Weston mutters my name in response against my lips. *Molly...Molly...*

In the back recesses of my mind, I hear voices.

Voices I choose to ignore.

That is, until the front door flies open and my brother yanks Weston back by the collar of his shirt and pushes him against the side of the house.

"You little fucker, get your goddamn hands off my sister," Matt angrily demands. Besides being absolutely humiliated, I can't read the expression on Weston's face, but I'm praying he doesn't take a swing at my brother. These hockey guys love nothing more than to beat the shit out of each other, and right now they're sizing each other up. Matt's hands are clenched at his sides, and he looks like he wants to punch Weston square between his eyes.

Although, to be honest, Weston looks a little out of it,

and I doubt he'd be of any use in a fight. He looks a little too turned on right now.

Matt turns to me with his hands in the air. "What the *fuck*, Molly?"

I roll my eyes at him. "Go inside the house, Matt. You are being ridiculous."

"You're out here practically humping this prick on Dad and Mom's porch, and you're calling *me* ridiculous?" His face is flush and it slowly begins to match his auburn hair. I always thought Matt was a big guy, but actually, now that they're standing side by side, he's no larger than Weston.

Before I can respond, Weston cuts in, stepping in front of me in a defensive move. "Okay man, that was totally uncalled for. We might have gotten a little carried away, but—"

Matt cuts him off, spitting mad, almost like he can't believe Weston has the balls to talk to him. "Who the *fuck* are you, anyway? Some hockey punk who's probably banging anything with a slit? I'm one of you." He thumps his chest with his fist. "I know how it works, and I *don't* want you near my sister."

"Jeez, Matt, can you watch your mouth? You're such an asshole." I shove him in the chest before crossing my arms over my chest and glaring at him. It's taking all my willpower not to call into the house for my dad. "You know what, Matt? Weston is a really nice guy, and as far as I'm aware, you're the only man-whore standing on this porch."

Here's the problem with these hockey players: they have to be very intuitive to be champions at the sport, and I know that even though they're both watching me, they've got their instincts homed in on each other.

"Can I just say something here?" Weston interrupts the evil glares Matt and I are giving each other. I groan.

"This better be damn good," Matt grumbles through clenched teeth.

"It's just...dude, I'm a *huge* fan."

15

Weston

> "My parents said we could be anything we wanted to be when we grew up, so Matthew became an asshole." – Molly

For a minute, Matthew Wakefield just stares back at me with the same green, albeit angrier eyes as his sister, the blood rushing back to his face. His shaggy, disheveled hair is in his face, but even so, just from the way he's looking at me, I can tell he's trying to decide if I'm being serious or if I'm being a sarcastic little prick. It's a little bit of both, actually, but one thing is for sure: two seconds ago he was ready to sucker punch me—I'd bet my left nut on that—and now he seems to at least be hesitating.

Matthew crosses his arms across his broad chest and doesn't respond.

"Yeah, sooo…I was at the game against Duke last year. That had to have been one of your best career games to date. That goal against Kuznetsov was one for the record books."

Matt purses his lips, but it's obvious the ego trip is softening his resolve, because his feet shift and he still hasn't hit me. Again, Molly groans, "Oh brother."

"What did you say your name was?" Matt asks, narrowing his eyes.

"McGrath. Weston." Before I can stop myself, my hand shoots out. "Good to meet you."

"I'm sure it is," he says with a sneer, not moving an inch.

Molly was right: Matt is an asshole.

"Matthew!" Molly shouts. "Oh my god, don't be so rude." She stands next to me and grabs the hand I have extended, her warm body sidling up against mine. Matt looks down at our clasped hands, and his wall goes back up.

Finally, he says, "I might have heard of you, kid. Must suck *dick* being compared to *me* all the time."

Slowly, I nod. "Yeah, but that only lasted my freshman year. That one year was all it took to break your high-scoring record." I plaster a smug look on my face, knowing I just royally pissed him off.

Matthew laughs with his head thrown back. "No fucking way you broke my record."

"Well, no, you're right. I didn't break it—I *decimated* it." Now it's my turn to laugh.

"You little fucker," Matthew mutters through gritted teeth, fists clenched at his sides. He takes a step forward.

"Hardly little, but...go on."

"STOP!" Molly shouts, pulling me by the hand toward the porch steps and pointing an angry finger at her dipshit brother. Wow, she is *pissed*. "Weston, *you* are leaving. Matt, get inside and find a good place to hide, because when I come back in, I'm going to *murder* you for ruining my night."

Molly

As I'm stalking across the turnaround, dragging Weston behind me, my freaking brother is standing on the front porch, shouting, "Don't think you're going to stand out there making out by your sex machine, McGrath. Are you listening? I'm watching you!"

Ugh, what an idiot.

I see my mom open the front door and drag him inside as he struggles against her grip. *Sheesh,* what the hell, Mom? It sure took her long enough to get that maniac out of my business. I'll have to thank her tomorrow, *one more time*, for telling Matt about my date in the first place.

I drag Weston behind the Hummer and thank god the driver's side door is away from the house, cloaked in the dark shadow of the truck. I shove him up against the huge black vehicle before giving his arm a good smack, grateful for the fact that no one can see us.

"What is wrong with you two?" I hiss as he shrugs with a lazy grin on his face. "That wasn't a pissing contest."

"Come here," he says quietly, the low timbre of his voice in the dark making my stomach flip-flop. Leaning up against his dad's shiny truck with his legs spread wide, Weston pats his hard thighs, inviting me to lean in. It all seems too…easy. Too comfortable. Too everything.

Shouldn't this be more—I don't know—*awkward*?

I feel like we've been doing this for...years.

Before I even think about what I'm doing, my body gravitates closer of its own accord, stopping just shy of his knees. Even in the dark, the sight of him stroking his legs while he watches me is erotic, and the butterflies return, wreaking havoc on my insides.

"What? You're crazy." I shake my head and cross my arms.

"Babe, you're so adorable when you're pissed. Come here," he repeats, grabbing my hand before I can protest, dragging me until I'm standing between those gorgeous thighs. I shake a little—I can't help it. This all is just too much for me to handle in one night. This large, sexy hunk of a guy, my dipshit brother...

And holy shit, back up—did he just call me *babe*?

"I should go before he comes back out and forces me to knock him on his ass." Weston's calloused hands are softly stroking my bare upper arms and he leans in, nuzzling my neck with his nose. It tickles and, sorry, but I *might* have giggled softly.

"Stop that. I'm mad at you both." Even as I say the words, I know they're a big fat lie, because I'm leaning into him too, lacing my fingers through his short hair. He moves his head around until he can plant a kiss in the palm of my hand.

"Aw, don't be mad, Molly..." His voice trails off playfully. "You make me feel so—"

"*McGrath, your time is up. Get the hell outa here. Molly, get your ass back in the house.*" Matthew's loud, annoying voice booms from the porch, and I vow to kill him in his sleep.

Weston's hands roam my backside, pulling me closer still. "Goddamn, he's a pain in the ass."

Ya think?

16

Molly

"Life is good? That's all you have to say about it? Unacceptable." – Jenna, the morning after

*L*et me tell you my ideal Sunday morning routine: wake up to the smell of frying bacon, typically around nine o'clock—or whenever I can pry my eyes open to the point where I'm functional. Most times, I'll open my laptop to check Facebook and surf the internet, or I'll just lie in bed awake and read—that is, until I decide it's finally time to change into something decent and wander downstairs to eat breakfast.

I know—rough life, right?

Now let me tell you what my ideal way to wake up on Sunday morning IS *NOT*: three hysterical teenage girls jumping on top of me, shaking me out of my slumber in a fit of giggles, but guess what—that's exactly how it goes down the day after my big date.

It's so loud in my room from all the shouting that I'm forced to cover my head with my blankets to block it out, which also serves to muffle my sudden cursing.

Huh, maybe I do take after Matthew after all…

I didn't think it could possibly get any more irritating, but I'm proved wrong when Jenna full-on hops up onto my bed, yanks off my comforter, and begins bouncing up and down. "Wake up, wake up, wake up!" she chants.

"Oh my god." I snap, *"Why are you here?"* I hurl my pillow at her but miss—by a long shot, I might add—then realize how counterproductive the move was.

Now I have no pillow.

"Get out of bed, slut, and tell us about your date," my friend Maddie deadpans, unceremoniously taking my desk chair and pulling it out. She flips her long blonde bangs out of her eyes, straddles the chair backward, and sits. "We waited all night for you to get home, so you can't kick us out."

"Yeah, I can't believe you didn't at least text one of us from a bathroom," Tasha chimes in, leveling me with an accusing stare. She takes a sip of her Starbucks chai latte—it's written on the side of her cup—and perches herself at the foot of my queen-sized bed. "That's girl code."

"Actually, Tasha, girl code is not dating your friend's ex-boyfriend…"

"Shut *up*, Maddie."

As I lay there, *freezing* in nothing but boxer shorts and a tank top with my bedding completely ripped off, I look around at my three friends and groan. Jenna is now sitting by my head and peering down at me with a smirk on her face. She's got on a full face of makeup, and yellow feather earrings wisp down to her shoulders. "We're not leaving, so you might as well sit up and start talking."

Everyone nods.

Jenna leans over so we're eye to eye. "Did he kiss you?"

Tasha immediately scoffs. "Of course he kissed her! Have you seen that guy? He's sex on a stick!"

This comment causes Maddie to raise her eyebrows and snort, loudly. "*Sex on a stick?* What the hell does that mean?"

"Oh my god, you guys, would you please stop? Just stop." I rub my temples with my forefingers and close my eyes. I know how excited they were for this date, and I know they're here because they love me, so I take a deep breath and let it out before saying, "It was really…a really… good date." *Hey, I don't want to lay all my cards out on the table at once.* Then they get all greedy.

Maddie rolls my desk chair closer to the bed and rests her arms on the back of the seat. "Where did he take you?"

"Do you guys mind if I get up and brush my teeth? I feel gross." I try to sit up so I can put my legs over the edge of the bed, but Jenna pushes me back down.

"Stay. You're a flight risk, and we're not taking any chances. Now spill."

"Jeez, at least let me sit up," I huff.

"Wait! Everyone wait!" Tasha throws her hands in the air, crisscrossing them like a referee. "Ladies. We forgot to ask one of the most important details. The detail that sets the whole scene…" She is at the foot of the bed but stretches herself out, leaning toward me with the intensity of a lioness stalking her prey. "What…were…you…wearing?"

What is it with girls and wardrobe selections? *Sheesh.* I bite the inside of my cheek to hold back the smile threatening to escape. Before I can talk, Jenna interrupts, talking rapidly. "She wore that white peplum top with dark skinnies and those high espadrille wedges. She looked smokin' hot. Okay, Molly. Go." She points her finger at me to indicate I should continue, but then Maddie interrupts.

"Were you showing boob?" She reaches over, grabs Tasha's latte, and takes a big sip, which earns her a loud, "Hey, give that back!"

Was I showing boob? I shrug. "Uh, I guess a little?"

"Nice." Maddie nods approvingly. "Did you see him checking out your cleeve?" Apparently, this is Maddie talk for *cleavage.*

I nod. "Yes, actually, and he wasn't the least bit embarrassed to get caught."

"Yeah, because he wanted to get his man-hands on 'em." She cackles and Tasha high-fives her.

"Okay, so where did he take you?" Jenna asks. "It was driving me crazy all night. Ugh, I still can't believe you didn't text."

I look around before answering, wringing my blanket between my hands because I know my response is going to put them all over the edge. I cover my ears before saying, "The Shedd Aquarium. We went downtown."

A chorus of very unladylike *shut the fuck up*s, *holy shit*s, and *oh em gee*s fill the room, plus lots of squeals and screaming. Once it dies down, Jenna silences the group with a "Shh, shh, shh. Oh my god. Oh my god. Amazing. I'm so super jealous." Her earrings float around her face, and even at nine in the morning, it strikes me how adorable she is. "*Damn,* that guy is good. I never would have guessed he had it in him."

Tasha snorts. "That's because he wants to have *it* in *her.*" Everyone laughs, including me—not that I don't think her words are embarrassing (my face is definitely bright red), but because sometimes I forget how clever she is.

"So what's he like? How did he treat you?" Jenna wants to know.

I think about this for a minute before answering, debating about how much to tell them and biting my lower lip in concentration. "He was great, *really* great—not at all like the image he puts out there. You know how he just always seems like he wants to be left alone? Well, he mostly does, but it's because he wants to get a hockey scholarship, not because he's an ass."

"Uh, Weston is in my gym class, and I'm going to have to disagree. That guy is an ass," Maddie says, pausing for effect. "A hot *piece* of ass!" She keels over laughing at her own joke, tipping the chair back and hitting Tasha in the leg.

"Get off me, you freak!" Tasha squeals, slapping Maddie on the arm and rolling her eyes. "Oh my god, you're so annoying."

"Well, anyway," I continue through their bickering, totally warming up to my topic. "We talked a lot. He has a sister who he's real protective of, and one who died when she was young. Her name was his first tattoo." Everyone gets quiet as they listen to me recount details. "So we went to the aquarium and sat for a long time in front of the jellyfish. It was real dark and peaceful. I mean, we didn't kiss or anything, but our legs were touching and it was still... electric, you know?"

"So then what?" Tasha whispers, probably because she doesn't want to spook me and have me clam up.

"So...then we left and he took me for ice cream. We stopped in River Hills, at that old fifties diner? Maddie, didn't you go there with Marshall once?" She nods. "Anyway, we sat at a corner table, even though there weren't any other people, and he ordered this huge sundae, like, extra *everything*, and I thought there was no way he could finish it."

"But he did."

I lie there looking at the ceiling, and for once my friends are quiet.

Waiting.

"Yeah, he did. I mean, the guy is huge—of course he's gonna finish it..." My voice trails off.

"Uh, just how *huge* is he, Molly?" Jenna cackles at her own perverted question.

I roll my eyes and say, "I wouldn't know."

"Well *that's* disappointing..."

"Okay, so what I really want to know is...do you think he'll ask you to Fall Formal? I mean, it's like next month," Jenna says, leaning over me again. You know what, until this very moment, I haven't considered Fall Formal. I haven't thought about the dance and if he would invite me...because if he *likes* me, wouldn't he maybe *want* to go? I can't help it; I'm a girl—we think about these things, even though I know it's not his thing, and he's never gone to a dance before...nor can I picture him at one, to be honest. In any case, a small seed of doubt plants and sprouts itself in my mind, and I'm wishing that Jenna hadn't brought it up, mostly.

On the other hand... I feel like I'm kind of past all of this and just want to move on, go to college, and be done with the whole high school scene.

"So what happened when he brought you home?" Maddie wants to know, changing the subject.

"Well, *you know...*" I can't stop the blush creeping up my neck.

"Was it any good? Did he stick his tongue down your throat?"

"Ugh, yeah, it was so good my toes were actually curling in my shoes, but then freaking Matthew came barging outside and ruined the whole moment."

"What!" There is a collective burst of outrage from my friends, and Jenna huffs, "You have got to be kidding me! Ugh, why is he such a jerkoff?"

"Is he here?" Tasha wants to know, rising from the bed. She's always had a major crush on him. In fact, when we were younger, she would only want to come over if Matthew was home. If he wasn't, she wouldn't even want to bother coming over, and I would go to her house. How messed up is that? "Do you think he's in his room?"

"No, stalker, sit down and get a grip. He has a game today. He probably left before the sun came up. His sole reason for coming home was to torture me and my date. It was so awful. I wanted to punch him between the eyes. Seriously, he came out onto the porch and started calling Weston all these names, embarassing the shit out of me."

"I'm sorry, Molly, but Matthew is *so* damn hot..." Tasha pouts, flopping back down onto the bed.

"Yup, can't argue with that one," Maddie agrees.

"Actually, I can argue with that," I say with a snort. "I'll be lucky if Weston calls me ever again. Matthew acted like he was committing a federal crime by putting his hands on me. I mean, he grabbed him by the shirt collar, for god's sake, and the worst part is my parents were inside the whole time and did nothing to stop him."

"Wait, wait—hold up. Go back to the part about the shirt collar—Weston wore a *dress* shirt? I think I'm going to pass out. Yup, I'm passing out," Jenna says, fanning herself with her hands then rolling on the bed until she's on top of me. We're all laughing hysterically. "Oh, girl, he must really like you."

"Yup," I say, rolling my eyes and giggling. "Nothing says love like a polo shirt."

17

Weston

> "I kind of just want someone who's going to like me for the total asshole I already am. It's less work." – overheard in the locker room

If you had told me a week ago I would be sitting in study hall anxiously watching the doorway for a girl to walk through it, I would have laughed my ass off and probably told you to shut the fuck up, but the joke's on me, because here I sit, covertly in the far corner, brim of my ball cap almost covering my eyes, willing Molly to walk through the door of the library.

Watching like a freaking sap.

I look up at the round clock hanging on the wall and curse because she technically only has a few more minutes to get here—two more minutes until the bell rings, actually—or I can write her off as having gone somewhere else for study hall.

A calculus book sits open in front of me, and my right

leg impatiently bounces up and down of its own free will as I watch the door like it's my job. The thought crosses my mind that I should have texted her telling her to meet me here, but I haven't gotten ahold of her since our date Saturday and don't want to seem too eager.

Too desperate.

The bell finally rings, and, disappointed that Molly hasn't shown up, I finally force myself to look down at my textbook. After staring at the same page for who knows how long, the words and numbers on the page still aren't making sense, and none of them are registering in my brain. I stare unblinking and trancelike down at the open pages, unable to stop thinking about our date, unable to stop thinking about Molly, who has been consuming my thoughts.

If my dad knew about those thoughts, he would personally serve my ass up on a silver platter and never let me see her again.

I know at least Mom was secretly excited for me; she was waiting up for me in the kitchen Saturday night to hear the details of my date with Molly. Actually, when I came into the house, she scared the shit out of me, sitting there in the dark on a barstool at the counter.

I might have even screamed a little.

I've actually never seen Mom that way before. My guess is that she holds a lot of it in because of my dad not wanting me to be serious about anything other than school and hockey, but really, she was pretty damn excited. I felt like a girl with the way she fussed over me, helping me get ready and insisting I get my shaggy hair trimmed earlier in the day—which of course, I did. And yeah, it was really fucking irritating, but I let her fuss anyway, because in a way I felt guilty. I know moms love that shit, and before this weekend, she's never had the opportunity.

I'll just keep telling myself all the effort was for my mom and sister, and not for Molly.

Speaking of Kendall, she got freakishly excited too, singing that annoying-ass song—"Weston and Molly sitting in the tree, K-I-S-S-I-N-G"—over and over before I bolted from the house.

Unable to concentrate, I lean back and take off my cap, running my fingers through the hair that's no longer there. I keep forgetting how short it is. Damn.

I raise my eyes as I set the hat down on my head, brim to the back, and I swallow hard as Molly walks into the room. She's stopped at the circulation desk, leaning over on her elbows across the counter with a slip of paper extended toward Mrs. Stalworth, the dumpy old librarian, who takes it and grins.

As they continue quietly chatting, I'm checking her out...

Obviously.

Even in casual school clothes, she makes my breath hitch, and I reach up to flip my hat back around so no one catches the expression in my eyes, which I'm assuming is akin to adoration. Let's just get something straight right now: Weston McGrath doesn't get caught checking chicks out—ever.

And just so we're clear, he also doesn't do girlfriends.

But hell, why is she so much goddamn cuter than I remember?

Molly leans against the counter, still oblivious to the fact that I'm watching her from the corner of the room. It's the first glimpse I've had of her since Saturday, and the sight of her gets my blood flowing, especially in those tight blue jeans, which hug her ass like a second skin.

She straightens to a stand, and my eyes rake hungrily over the navy blue and white striped tank top that's pulled tightly across her breasts (*nice*), over which she's wearing an unbuttoned gray cardigan. A thin brown leather belt is wrapped around her waist, and her hair is pulled back into a ponytail with the cutest fucking white bow in it.

Now how in the hell am I going to concentrate?

Finally she turns and scans the room, looking for a place to sit. I sit at attention, my posture a little straighter, and silently will Molly to notice me in the back of the room. Shit, why did I have to sit back here? Oh, that's right, because I'm a *fucking idiot*.

Patiently, I wait.

I'm rewarded when our eyes meet and she takes those first tentative steps toward me—but then she falters. Biting on her lower lip, she is obviously measuring whether or not to approach me, and I mentally chastise myself for not having texted her after our date. It was a great date—so great I was hard for two days afterward—but let's be honest, this isn't going anywhere. Despite that, I feel like a world-class jackass, and I wouldn't blame her if she sat somewhere else, even though I know she won't.

Because Molly Wakefield is classier than that, and I doubt she tolerates bullshit. In fact, I would kind of expect her to waltz over and bitch me out for not calling.

Weaving her way through the tables that have been staggered around the room, I think she is going to come over to my table.

Then she shocks the crap out of me.

In a library full of people, instead of choosing to sit with me, she parks it at a table with some random emo chick I've never seen before and who is wearing all black. Her chair is facing me, and she shoots me a smile that I can tell is forced even from here, despite my lack of a sensitivity gene. Molly then lobs her black backpack onto the table's surface in front of her, and I watch as she unzips it and takes out a notebook then a calculator.

Fine, ignore me. See if I give two shits.

I glance at the clock. Forty minutes left in the period. I can handle that.

Only…I keep stealing glances at Molly, who has her head bent, the ends of her ponytail flirting with her collarbone. The little bow pinned in her hair is a nice contrast to the tight fit of her shirt, and my eyes wander to the bare skin above her neckline.

Staring at her neck reminds me of how fantastic she smells, how her smooth skin tasted against my tongue, and I shift in my seat, the memories making me hard—in the damn library, of all places. Watching her sit there, completely ignoring me like I'm not even in the room, is bringing out all of my narcissistic tendencies, and now all I want is her attention.

I really am a fucker.

Yup, that's right—my resolve lasted all of five minutes.

Look up, Molly, I quietly chant to myself. *Look up.*

And then on cue, as if she can hear me, she does.

Molly

He's got my attention. Now what's he going to *do* with it?

I watch as Weston stares me down, and to say I'm totally confused right now is an understatement. For two whole days I waited for him to contact me—they felt like a freaking eternity. I carried my phone around pitifully because I didn't want to miss that ping of a text alert or a phone call, hoping it would be him and being let down and disappointed each time it wasn't.

Not only that, I lay in bed pathetically both nights until my eyes drooped, waiting for my phone to light up in the dark. Every new friend request on Facebook could have been him but wasn't.

Waiting. Sucked.

All I keep thinking is, *Gee, Molly, you let him stick his tongue down your throat, for crying out loud.*

But you know what *else* sucks? The fact that I don't know who to be more pissed off at: him for blowing me off, or me for letting it affect me so much.

I *really* thought—ugh, crap, you *know* what I thought.

Why do guys have to ruin everything with their melodramatic bull crap? I mean seriously. It's not like I wanted to skip down the halls with him holding hands, but a text or something would have been nice. A simple *Thanks for the date* would not have been too much to ask and would have taken him all of what, ten seconds?

Can I also point out that guys have the nerve to call *girls* dramatic when they're just as bad? I know exactly what Weston McGrath is thinking in that fat head of his. He's worried I'm going to unleash my inner stalker and fall madly in love with him when he doesn't have time for it, which reminds me—I once innocently asked this guy,

Dave, to a baseball game, and instead of just telling me no like a normal human being, he said he wasn't looking for a relationship, so yeah, there's your proof that guys are just as bad as girls.

And for the record: I'm not saying I wouldn't fall in love with Weston…because I'm already halfway there.

I'm guess I'm disappointed it was just that one date.

The one date that ruined me for everyone else.

How annoying.

Weston

I don't know how to fix this.

Molly is still watching me from her table a few rows over, sporting an impassive expression if I've ever seen one. She raises an eyebrow, silently daring me to make a move.

I hesitate.

Then, in what some might consider a dick move, I push the chair opposite me out with the toe of my boot, sliding it away from the table in a silent invitation.

A plea, in my own twisted way, for her to come sit with me.

Leaning back in my seat and crossing my arms, I try to appear unaffected as I gauge her reaction. At first she narrows her eyes; obviously, she's trying to figure out why I pushed the chair out. Hell, *I'm* trying to figure out why I pushed the chair out when two minutes ago I was in panic mode about relationships.

So this could have just become one of those awkward moments in my life that I don't know how to handle. What I'd really like to do is walk out of study hall to avoid the entire situation, but I won't be able to without getting my ass chewed out by the librarian or earning myself a detention. Damn, I hate second-guessing myself. Would it have killed me to be friendlier when she was looking for a place to sit? The very least I could have done was offered up a smile, but at the time I was still trying to decode what her sitting with me might mean.

Shit, that sounded like something a girl would say.

Now…*she's too far away*.

At least it doesn't appear she hates me. Still studying me, Molly starts tapping her pen on the cover of her book—I can hear it from here—until the goth chick at her table reaches out, grabs it out of her hands, and tosses it on the carpeted ground.

Molly looks stunned. I watch as her neck turns bright red, and I swear, if I weren't trying to get back into her good graces, I would be laughing my ass off right now.

Stop being a pussy, Weston, and get in there, my dad's voice echoes in my head. It's a mantra I've heard thousands of times, and I've never repeated it to myself until now. So, hooking my booted foot back around the leg of the chair I've just pushed out, I pull it back in…then push it back out, giving her a pointed look.

Her eyebrows raise and she cocks her head.

"*Come here*," I mouth quietly.

Indignantly, Molly purses her lips, but even so, the corners are upturned…the little brat.

"*Please?*" Begging in the library—I feel like such a

douche.

It only takes a few more seconds before Molly is biting down on her lower lip and letting go of her own demons long enough to collect her things slowly and stand. My eyes roam her body as she walks toward me. I think I just realized I could look at her all day and it would never get old.

Her hip comes to rest on the corner of my library table as she stands in front of me with a hand on one waist, hip jutted out. "Let's get one thing straight, mister," she whispers, still vertical. "I'm not one of your rink bunnies. I won't worship at your feet, and I'm certainly not gonna—"

I grab her hand and pull her in for a quick peck on the lips to shut her up. "Sit down already, would you?"

It does the trick; she plops down in the seat I kicked out. Molly glares at me—hey, at least she's here—before making a show of digging through her backpack. Since I'm new at this whole thing, I genuinely wonder how long she's going to keep ignoring me, despite the fact that she's now seated at my table.

I don't have to wonder long.

"You really hurt my feelings," she whispers across the table without looking up from the open notebook in front of her.

"How?" Sorry, but I'm clueless. I mean…I might have something of an inkling, but come on, people, it's not like two days is exactly a lifetime to wait for a phone call.

"Because, *jackass*, I put myself out there and you couldn't get ahold of me?" Molly puts down her pen and levels me with her bright green eyes blazing. "Look, it's fine if you aren't interested, but just say so."

I push the ball cap back on my forehead and lean over slowly so we're eye to eye. "Oh, I'm definitely interested." I can tell by looking at her that her heart rate accelerates; her pupils dilate and her cheeks immediately get pink. Then I make her laugh when I say, "Want me to prove it to you by carrying your books to your locker?"

Molly shakes her head back and forth but does nothing to hide her grin. "Why do I have the feeling you're going to be a pain in my ass?" She gasps as her hand flies up to her mouth, obviously mortified that she swore in front of me.

Big deal. Like I care.

"Yeah, probably, but I bet you'll like it." I shrug. "Hey, do you have any food in your bag?"

Nodding, she drags her backpack across the table and reaches her arm in, feels around, and then blindly pulls out a bag of cashews and a granola bar. "You seem…hungry a lot. Is food all you think about?"

I grab the granola bar and tear into the wrapper with my teeth while she stares slack-jawed. "Uh, *yeah*—well, that and sex."

18

Molly

"The thing about guys is *we* have to tell them what they want, and that's bible. You should probably write that down somewhere." – Maddie

My legs feel kind of wobbly when the bell finally rings and we make our way down the hall.

I can hardly believe Weston is walking behind me, let alone walking me to my locker. The heat from his hand on the small of my back imprints on my skin as he guides me along through the crowded hallway, and strangely enough, he seems to know exactly where he's going—like he's been to my locker before.

The few times I get jostled by the sea of people, Weston's large hand comes around and grips my waist to steady me, and it does terrible things to my insides. We reach my locker, and after I dial the combination and pull open the small metal door, he leans forward and says near my ear, "I can't really stick around. I should get to practice, or Coach will chew my ass out for being late."

I shiver and nod my head, barely comprehending. What warm-blooded female could concentrate with his hot breath near their ear? "Jesus, don't do that," I mumble.

"Do what?" his low voice rumbles again.

I turn to face him, and I've put us in a position where his lips are now inches from mine. "We've been on *one* date. Don't you think panting all over each other in the hallway is moving a little fast?"

"Uh, no? Panting is only the start of what I want to do with you."

"Who talks like that? We're in high school." I give him a smack then let my hand linger from his bicep back up to his broad shoulder. In typical guy fashion, Weston flexes his muscles. "Ugh, you're so…"

"Sexy?"

"I was going to say ridiculous…but yeah, you're sexy too." I turn toward my locker and start putting books in.

"Hmm, can't say any girl has ever called me ridiculous before, but I guess I can see it. Want to have *noodles* with me tonight?"

I turn back around to face him and wrinkle my nose. "See, now when you say noodles like that—definitely *not* sexy."

Weston laughs and reaches for me, his large hand spanning my waist. "Shit, you get me so worked up and you don't even try."

I groan because I cannot honestly believe I'm standing here having this conversation. "If I say yes to noodles, will you leave me alone and go to practice?"

"Yes, but first you have to—"

"Well now, isn't this cozy. Not wasting any time, Weston?"

Weston

The snarky voice that interrupts us belongs to none other than Alexis Peterson. She's standing across the hallway, shooting daggers at Molly's back, one hand propped on her hip in a defensive stance. For the life of me, I don't know why any girl who wants to date me would get all up in my shit like it's any of her damn business.

Not to mention, the snotty comment just makes me think she's a petty bitch, and the fact that she did it in front of Molly makes me want to punch a locker.

Jealousy doesn't become her.

Actually, jealousy doesn't become anyone, but really, what are you going to do about it?

"What's up, Alexis?" I ask through clenched teeth, ignoring her sarcastic remark. I'm going to pretend she didn't just give me a verbal putdown in front of Molly. Because she's staring at us so intently, I ask, "Did you have something you wanted to say to me?" *Before I go ape shit on your ass?*

Instead of answering me, Alexis just stands there and sizes Molly up, doing a visual inventory of her clothes, hair, and makeup. Based on the curl in her lip, she obviously finds her lacking. Ah, so she's crazy *and* blind. "He's just using you," she finally blurts out, directing her comment at Molly. She seems awfully satisfied with herself.

"What the fuck, Alexis?" She has some nerve.

I take a step forward.

Instead of reacting like the typical female and getting all pissed off like I expect her to, Molly lays the palm of her hand on my chest to calm me down. Standing her ground, she turns her back to Alexis and takes a denim jacket out of her locker. In no rush, she shrugs into it, flips her long ponytail over the collar, and adjusts the cuffs. Finally turning, Molly smiles kindly and weighs her words. "You know, I appreciate your concern, but I think I'll take my chances."

This girl is incredible. I want to grab her and kiss her, but Crazy Eyes is watching us.

I notice the smile doesn't reach Molly's eyes.

Closely watching Alexis, I'm *pretty* sure she wants to lunge at both of us like an alley cat. Who the hell would purposely date this chick, let alone sleep with her? (Word is, she gets around.) Actually, I can think of a few people, but that's not my point. Her eyes widen in a slightly wild way while her face contorts and turns a shade of beet red.

And hey, what's with her clenching her fists at her sides?

"You know, Alexis, you might want to consider an anger management program…" This is my attempt at humor—no applause necessary.

Molly smacks my arm, ignoring the murderous glares coming from the blonde across the hall, and gives me a gentle nudge before saying, "Go or you'll be late. I can handle this." She nods her head toward Alexis.

Oh shit. That can't be good…can it?

I want to lean in to kiss her forehead, but I refrain. "Okay…I guess I'll see you later, then."

She nods.

With the corner of my eye trained on Crazy Alexis, I saunter off down the hallway, glancing back only once to catch a glimpse of Molly crossing her arms.

Molly

"I've never had an issue with you, Alexis. What's the problem?" I'm not stupid—I know what her problem is with me, just like I know she's been chasing after Weston and… from the looks of her, she's got psycho tendencies.

I shut my locker door and hoist my backpack over my shoulder before crossing my arms and planting my right foot on the ground, steeling myself for whatever she's about to say. Let me remind you that I'm no stranger to confrontation—*hello*, I was raised with *Matthew,* who did nothing but start fights growing up. Yeah, I can hang with the best of them. Regardless, who in their right mind wants to get in an altercation at school *over some guy?*

This hasn't ever really happened to me, even with Jenna and my other friends. We just don't squabble like this, and to be honest, I guess I'm only still standing here because I'm curious to see where all this is going.

Doesn't she realize Weston isn't even my boyfriend? If he were, well, then I guess we really would have an issue with her standing in front of me like this.

"I just wanted to let you know that he uses people."

This is news to me.

"Oh yeah? How so?"

"Are you kidding? Hello! He sleeps with everyone!" Her voice is elevated, and I'm not sure she's even trying to remain calm.

"*Everyone,* you say? Wow, that's a lot of people, Alexis. So...has he slept with *you*?"

She huffs indignantly. "I'm not a *slut* like *some* people."

Uh, did she just insinuate that I'm a slut?

"Oh, so he's slept with everyone, just not with you." I snap my fingers and point at her, even though I know it's rude. "I get it. Is that why you're pissed off? Because to be honest"—I glance down at my watch—"I have other shit I could be doing right now instead of standing here watching you throw a temper tantrum."

"You are such a *bitch*."

I roll my eyes. She's so absurd.

"You know what? Weston is *just* a guy, Alexis. Just. A. Guy. And one you aren't even dating." I wave my arm in that way that says *whatever*. "Ugh, whatever—be pissed. I'm leaving—unless of course you have something *else* you'd like to say, since you have *yet* to blow me away with your observations."

Oh wow—I really *am* a bitch.

Shaking my head, I head off down the hallway—though not before whipping out my cell phone to call Jenna.

Hey, I'm only human, and this is too good to resist gossiping about.

19

Weston

"Thing about an itch is eventually you're gonna have to scratch it." – Tate Myers, River Glen Hockey Center

For the life of me, I cannot concentrate during hockey practice, and I'm lucky I made it through without anyone noticing my lack of focus. I mean, I missed almost every shot I made on the goalie, for Christ's sake. As much as I hate to admit it, my sole mission—for the first time in my hockey career—is to get done and get out so I can meet Molly for dinner.

I'm itching to see her again, and literally tripping into my pants after practice might not have been my proudest moment, or my smoothest, but this…this *thing* we've got going on is new to me, and after today I will be the first person to admit I'm definitely liking it.

Dare I even admit to liking the sarcastic and insulting commentary in the locker room from my teammates? Apparently, they all knew I had a date this weekend and whom it was with, thanks to Rick. Luckily I didn't feel the urge to hit anyone when Lee Brickner spent the entire afternoon referring to me as Cupcake. (Okay, that's a lie—I *did* want to hit someone, just not as hard as I normally would want to.)

See, what Brickner doesn't realize is that in some sick fucked up way, I kind of liked the teasing.

I haul ass on my bike to Kyoto, which I've already subconsciously categorized as *our* place, and my body hums to life when I spot Molly's Jeep already sitting in the parking lot. Shifting down gears, I pull into the parking spot next to her. Through the plexiglass face guard on my motorcycle helmet, I can see her head bent, texting behind the wheel. She looks up and smiles just as I remove my headgear and give my head a shake, running my fingers through my still damp hair.

We meet on her side of the Jeep, and childishly I give the small white bow in her hair a tug. "Hey," is my lame greeting.

She rolls her eyes. "Hungry?"

Hell-freaking-yes, I think, while also wanting to skip dinner entirely to make out. Molly's an amazing kisser, not to mention just thinking about sucking on her neck again is making me hard. I shift uncomfortably as if she can read my debauched mind.

Actually, I don't think she would be shocked, let alone care. I'm sure she's heard worse from that tit-wad brother of hers.

In no time at all, we're sliding into a red vinyl booth—the same booth where we first met—and I'm even hungrier than I was five minutes ago. Not one to shy away from stuffing my face full, I take my fork and twist up a big wad of noodles, not giving them time to cool before shoving them in my mouth.

They're hot as hell, and I panic as I reach for my cup of soda, not wanting to look ridiculous.

Too late.

Molly tries smirking at me, but her pert nose slightly scrunches up as she bites back a laugh. "Oh, so you think that's funny?" I ask her while running my tongue back and forth along my teeth to ease the pain on my taste buds. *Maybe she should kiss it and make it better,* I can't stop myself from thinking. "I wouldn't be giggling at you if you burnt *your* tongue."

Yes, I'm whining.

Molly thinks about this for a bit before she says thoughtfully, her empty fork suspended in the air, "You know, I would pay actual paper money to see you giggle."

"*Paper* money? Wow. I bet you would."

"Yeah, I would."

We stare at each other, and I narrow my eyes before digging into my noodles again. Molly bends her head to twirl a bite onto her fork then holds it up to her lips, blowing air over the top of it to cool it down. I stare at her little bow-shapped mouth as she does to her dinner what I suddenly want her doing to me—and thank God I don't say this shit out loud.

I'd look like *the* biggest asshole.

The noodles are still steaming hot, and I immediately gulp down another drink of ice-cold soda. I let my mouth hang open for a few seconds, opening and closing my jaw to speed along the cooling process.

Molly shakes her head and her lips curls up. "Why do guys always do that?"

"Do what?"

I watch as she rolls her eyes. "Eat scalding-hot food that burns their taste buds off."

"You seriously have to ask that?" She stares at me blankly. "Because we're *starving*, that's why."

She shakes her head sadly. "I will never understand guys. That's why I never date."

Okay, now I'm confused. "Uh…if you don't date, then what is this?" My index finger points back and forth between both our bodies of its own accord as I lazily suck through the straw of my drink. It falls out of my mouth as lift my head to wait for her response.

"I…I… It's just…noodles?"

"So?" I watch as her face gets bright red, and in a gesture I've never seen her execute, she reaches up and twirls the end of her ponytail around her finger and bites down on her lip before looking me directly in the eyes. "Didn't you hear? Noodles are the key to my heart."

Molly only hesitates for a second before groaning. "You did *not* just say that."

"I did. In fact, I was hoping for a more enthusiastic response, so unfortunately for you, I will *not* be making out with you at the end of this date—or non-date. Whatever." I know I'm stupidly grinning, but the look on her face is priceless. Her green eyes have gotten huge, and now she's gaping at me with her mouth hanging open.

I eat a few forkfuls of vegetables before slowly speaking the next few words.

"You know, Molly, you're not at all like I was expecting you to be that day I was checking you out in the library." Still no sound comes out of her, so I continue. "You looked so ridiculously cute." *And sexy in that skirt.* "Uh, why are you looking at me like that?"

She shakes her head like she's shaking feathers out. "I'm sorry, I just... I'm surprised, that's all. It's not a bad thing." A smile tugs at the corner of her mouth, but she's totally fighting it.

"Can I ask you something?" I push the noodles around in my bowl and watch her from the corner of my eye. She nods as she takes a sip of her water. "What were you thinking about when you looked up?"

She thinks about it before answering. "Do you want me to be honest with you, or should I lie?"

"Well, if you're about to say you wanted to get naked, then say whatever you want." I waggle my eyebrows to punctuate my sentence and shoot her one of my toothy, megawatt grins that girls go crazy for.

"Well, not exactly. I was a little...freaked out. I mean, it's not like you have this sterling reputation. I thought you were a jerk—or I mean, that's what I'd heard."

I consider this information. "Huh. Well that sucks. I like my version better."

Finally she throws her head back and laughs. "The naked Molly version? Figures."

"Uh, I bet naked Molly looks incredible. Let's see, if I close my eyes I can almost picture it..." I squint my eyes closed and pretend to be searching for a visual. "Yup. *Oh yeah*, there it is. Nice..."

Molly's laugh is airy and light as she hits my arm.

"Knock it off, Weston. Stop trying to picture me with no clothes on."

"Fine, but only because there's something I need to ask you. Well, more like tell you—" I'm interrupted by the sound of a feminine voice calling out, "Hey, Wes, what's up?" It causes both Molly and me to crane our necks to see two girls from school—I think their names might be Mary and Olivia, but that's just a guess—approaching our table. They're both wearing backpacks and have their cell phones out, so one can assume they're at Kyoto to study. The blonde (Olivia?) has ear buds in and is slightly bobbing her head as she walks toward us.

Now, I'm not sure what possesses people who hardly know me to greet me with such familiarity, but they do, and I'm irritated. So, by the time they're done dodging and weaving through the sparsely attended dining room and arrive at our booth, my leg is bouncing under the table. Maybe you've already noticed, but this is a habit of mine when I'm annoyed or nervous.

The girls bounce up to the table—yeah, bounce—with the one called Mary (I think) taking the lead. I notice—only because her shirt is too small—that she's got big boobs and she's sticking them out. *Dear God, how obvious can you be?*

I shift in my chair, knowing this is going to be awkward.

"Hi, Wes. How's it going?" Big Boobs Small Shirt is now standing at the corner of our table, eyes trained on me with a huge smile on her face. It's creepy, and I shift my gaze to Molly, who is eating noodles with a smirk on her face. Her eyes are crinkled at the corners, and I get the feeling that she's secretly laughing at me.

She is going to be no help at all in getting these two away from me.

"It's going fine." I give the girl a vague answer, hoping if I'm curt enough she'll leave.

"Gosh, do you eat here a lot?" Like I'm going to walk into that trap by answering *that* question. Instead, I grunt and say nothing.

"I saw your bike outside. Are you going to ride it home in this rain?" the other girl asks, playing with the strap on her backpack. She's mousy, and it's quite obvious she's Big Boobs' yes-girl. You know, everyone has that one friend who goes along with everything they say, always fading into the background, never stealing the spotlight for herself.

"It's raining?" Molly breaks in.

"Yeah. Just started. Just a drizzle though." How did I not know it was going to rain?

"If you need a ride home, Wes, my mom lent me her car," Big Boobs Small Shirt says with hope in her voice, again using my first name like she knows me.

I snort. "Yeah, like I want to climb into your mom's minivan when my date here has a perfectly good Jeep."

There.

That ought to give them a hint. To really amp up the jerk factor and to be a bigger prick, I stuff my face with a fork full of food and chew with my mouth open. It's pretty revolting if I do say so myself.

I can't force myself to look at Molly.

She's got to be totally disgusted with me right now.

"This is a date? Like, you're on a date?" Big Boobs'

sidekick asks.

"That's what I said, isn't it?"

"So, do you date other people, or just her?"

"Um, excuse me, 'her' is sitting right here and she has a name," Molly says, the irritation in her voice palpable.

"Just her," I grind out.

"Oh." Big Boobs sounds crestfallen, and her shoulders slump. She starts biting her lip, oblivious to the fact that her trusty sidekick keeps clearing her throat behind her. Then a thought must occur to her, because she perks up again. "So are you taking her to Fall Formal?"

Okay, now I'm one hundred percent pissed off. My dating status is none of their fucking business, and I'm suddenly furious they're asking me these questions in front of Molly. If we were out on the ice, I'd take Big Boobs Small Shirt by the facemask and lay her out flat on the ice. However, my only recourse is to calmly lay down my fork and clasp my hands in front of me on the table. I can feel my nostrils flaring. "Uh, *no*, I'm *not* taking her to Fall Formal, not that it's any of your business. You might not know this, but I don't have time for that kind of kiddie bullshit." I pause. "Now, are you done interrogating me, or should we wait until my food is completely cold before you walk away?"

And *that,* ladies and gentleman, is how I got my reputation as a complete asshole.

Molly

20

"The last time I condoned 'the wet look' was when I was five, and even then it was hideous." – Tasha

There are moments in your life when you just want to crawl under the table and hide.

This, ladies and gentleman, is one of those moments.

Weston sits across the table from me, watching Mary Rogers and her best friend, Olivia, shrink away to their own table. If they had a massive crush on him before, he sure went and ruined it with his ugly tirade. I'll admit it: even though the words weren't directed at me, they were *about* me, and they hurt.

Did I want to go to Fall Formal?

Not really.

I mean, we've covered this topic before. However, not wanting to go and having the guy you like completely repulsed by the idea of taking you?

Um, *yeah*, two totally different things.

Now I'm faced with the question: how do I react to all this? There he sits, his face finally going back to its normal color after being beet red, totally ignorant of my hurt feelings.

I push some rice around my plate with a knife, having completely lost my appetite. Quietly I say, "*Wow*. You really are an asshole."

Weston looks up at me from his plate, surprised. "What did I do?" I tap the knife on the table before setting it down; my stomach feels like it has been twisted in a thousand little knots. Weston's brow furrows and he asks again, "What? Molly…"

I bite my lip, uncertainty fueling my next move. Awkwardly, I grasp for my jacket while at the same time grabbing my purse. Weston reacts stealthily, reaching across the table in a futile attempt to stop me. "What are you doing?" The low timbre of his confused voice almost has me hesitating as it vibrates and warms my core, but I've gone this far already, and I'm not stopping until I'm in the parking lot.

Are guys really so stupid?

Does he really not know what he said to upset me?

I weave my way through Kyoto, sights set on the door. It's getting dark out, and the visibility in the parking lot is terrible; the rain that's pouring down outside makes it almost impossible to see my Jeep from the door.

Good.

It would serve that A-hole right having to hitch a ride with Mary Rogers, who apparently got dressed in the dark this morning and couldn't find anything but a toddler's T-shirt to cover her giant boobs.

Or better yet, maybe he can call that jackass Rick Stevens to come pick him up.

You know what they say: one giant jackass deserves another. (Actually, I just made that up, but it fits, don't you think?)

I shrug into my jacket, thankful that it has a hood, and continue standing in the doorway of the restaurant, watching the rain come down in sheets. In the distance, lightning flashes, and my hand grips the door handle. It's coming down so hard I have to psych myself up and count to three before I can make myself push the door open. Then, just as I'm about to give the door a shove, a large, warm hand covers my shoulder.

Of course I know who it is. I don't even bother turning around.

"Can we talk about this?" His voice is inches from my ear. "Please. Let's go sit down."

I am too embarrassed and hurt to go back into the dining room. "Weston, just let me leave. You really… That was…" I shake my head and stare into the parking lot.

"Fine. Then let's go out to your car." He shoves the door open with the toe of his boot and envelops my hand in his, pulling me unceremoniously out into the pouring rain.

"SHIT SHIT SHIT!" I screech as we run to my car, water pelting our faces and splashing under our feet. Vainly, I thank God my hood is up and that my hair is staying dry. It's gotten cold, and I can feel my shoes and pant legs getting soaked.

"Keys!" he shouts when we get to the Jeep. I fumble in my pocket, finally slapping them into his outstretched palm. Several seconds later, he's opening the door to the driver's seat and ushering me inside before jogging around to the passenger side.

Side by side in the dry shelter of my car, we shake ourselves off, both of us shucking off our rain-soaked jackets. The pounding on the roof is loud, and quarters inside the Jeep are so close that an intimate atmosphere is created inside the cab that isn't normally there. Weston's large body sits next to me, and suddenly I'm aware of his every breath. He swipes his large hand over his hair a few times before letting it fall to his thigh.

He turns his head to look at me and exhales. "This could take a while to pass. You want me to call someone to pick me up?"

I consider this and slowly shake my head. "No. Let's see what happens, I guess. I probably shouldn't be driving around in this either." I let my neck relax back onto the headrest and stare up at the canvas roof, quickly praying to the waterproof gods that it doesn't leak any time soon.

"So…I guess since we're stuck here we might as well…you know, talk about what an ass I was back there."

"I thought guys hated talking."

"Yeah, about *our* feelings maybe, but not yours. On second thought, I've been doing a lot of shit lately that's out of character, so what the hell do I know." Weston shrugs and leans his brawny frame against the door. He has on a ratty old muscle shirt that actually has tons of rips and holes in it like Freddy Krueger got ahold of it, but it's not bothering me one bit because it's affording me glimpses of the smooth skin underneath.

A shirt that I'm itching to run my fingers under…to

feel the smooth skin I'm itching to run my fingers *over*.

Embarrassed that I'm starting to picture him, um, *you know*, I clear my throat and look out the window. "I get that you were annoyed with Mary and Olivia, but…it was kind of embarrassing when you were so…"

"Rude?"

"No. When you were so…"

"Such an asshole?"

"No!" *Oops*, I think as I let a chuckle slip out. "Would you let me finish?" *Honestly, he is worse than Jenna with this interrupting.* "Look. I'll just say this: I have no plans to go to any dances, with you or anybody, but seriously, did you have to sound so disgusted about it in front of Mary and Olivia? First they're talking about me like I'm not there, then you go and get all pissed off when they ask about Fall Formal. We all get it: Weston doesn't do dances."

There. I got it all out without sounding whiny.

"Is that it? That's why you got all huffy?"

"Uh, yeah. That pretty much sums it up." I cross my arms and purse my lips. "And to be honest, Weston, I was hoping for a more *enthusiastic* response…so unfortunately for you, I will *not* be making out with you at the end of this date—or non-date."

His eyebrows shoot up as I throw the words he spoke earlier back in his face with a soft smile on my face.

"Is that *so*?" His question is slow and deliberate, with a silent suggestion to it that makes me tingle a little in my girly parts.

"Yup."

Weston eyes me silently with no expression on his face, his stare focusing on my lips a heartbeat too long before he says, "Okay, Molly, then I guess I have no choice but to just lie back for a bit and take a short nap until this rain passes." He feigns a yawn. "Took a real pounding in practice today and I. Am. Beat." He reaches for the side lever to recline the seat and lies back, crossing those beautiful arms across his broad chest, the tattoo on his right arm a stark contrast to the white of his shirt. "Want to rub my back? I can turn over…"

Seriously?

Is this a joke?

Because even though not five minutes ago I was pissed off at him, all I can think about now is getting my hands on him—*and he's choosing to take a nap.*

I sit ramrod straight in the driver's seat, staring at his strong arms, not really knowing what to do.

21

Weston

"I don't even want to know what's going through that thick skull of yours." – Brian Mcgrath

I have to bite my lip so the grin doesn't escape. I can literally feel Molly watching me from her side of the car, even though my eyes are closed. I just know she's sitting there, overanalyzing the situation, when really all I want to do is get her in my lap. Feel her under my palms. Kiss her neck.

It's that plain and simple.

I hear her shift beside me, and I lazily let my eyelids creep open. "Stop staring at me," I drone, knowing damn well it's going to spook her. She says nothing, but Molly's eyes get real wide because I caught her red-handed, and her head whips around to look back out the front window. Presented with her profile, I'm given a side view of that perky little bow in her hair, and I smile despite myself.

I decide to put her out of her misery. "It's not that I wouldn't want to take you to Fall Formal, Molly. It's that I *can't*."

She turns to face me, confusion marring her brow. "It's fine, Weston. You don't have to explain yourself. I mean, it's not like I'm your…" Her voice trails off as I tuck my arms behind my head. Her green eyes linger on my bare upper arms, then down over my armpits, and finally down my torso. Her perusal is turning me on and let's face it, it's taking every ounce of willpower I possess to remain still and not just reach over and grab her.

Lord knows I want to.

I sit up and reach to pull the seat back to a sitting position.

The silence hangs over her unfinished sentence as those last few words sink in. *I mean, it's not like I'm your…girlfriend.* She was obviously about to say it, and suddenly, this is a moment of clarity for me. That unspoken word has got my mind working.

I let it marinate inside my brain.

"My Uncle Leo is getting married in Chicago at Millennium Park that day, and I'm an usher." A little O forms on Molly's mouth as the words sink in, followed by a slow grin that settles on her lips. Good, I've managed to surprise her. "So obviously I can't go to Fall Formal." By the way, thanks, Uncle Leo, because I wouldn't have gone to the dance anyway, but Molly doesn't need to know that.

22

Molly

> "Seriously, one of the top five reasons to own a car is so you can make out in it. I'm pretty sure I read that somewhere." – Jenna

That's it—he's going to a wedding. He's not repulsed by the thought of taking me out in public, and he's not ashamed to be seen with me at a school function. I let this new information process inside my brain, and my insides fill with warmth again. All of the rejection and embarrassment I felt a few minutes earlier have fled as fast as they arrived, and I survey Weston with a new appreciation.

I feel…overjoyed.

Ecstatic.

Giddy.

Suddenly, he's all the more attractive, and who'd have thought that could even be possible?

The silence—well, technically it's not at all silent, because the noise from the rain continues to fill the cab of my

Jeep with the sound of tiny, banging drums—is too much for me, so I reach forward and take a pack of gum out of the cup holder, offering one to Weston. "Would you like a piece?"

"Sure. Actually, can I have two? One can never be too fresh."

"Of course." I take two sticks out and unwrap them, setting them in his open palm. Without even meaning to, I let my fingers linger before taking my hand away.

"Mmm, mint makes me sleepy." Weston lets out a short yawn and pats his mouth before popping the gum inside. "Long day." He gives me a look and smiles before closing his eyes, chewing slowly.

"You're not seriously going to take a nap, are you?" *Because I seriously don't think I would be able to stand it.* Sitting in this small car with him so close is…well, I'll just say it: it's making me want to climb into his lap and kiss him all over. Even the sound of him breathing is making me hot.

"Why, did you have something else in mind?" He's smirking with his eyes closed.

Perfect.

I do have something else in mind, but I'm not saying so out loud. "Um…not really." *Liar, liar, pants on fire.*

"Really?" He opens his eyes and looks at me, the skepticism written all over his face. He looks at my lips before saying, "That's strange, because I can think of a few hundred things to do right now, and they *definitely* all involve parts of your body." He chuckles to himself and I shiver. "Don't hate me for saying so."

I dig deep inside myself to summon the inner Jenna

who seems to want to come out, and I only falter a split second before murmuring, "So what are you going to do about it?"

Weston looks at me with his eyes wide and says slowly, "I'm sorry, did you just beg me to make out with you, or am I losing my hearing?"

I slap the steering wheel and laugh. "I am *not* begging you to make out with me. I was just being...suggestive."

Weston sits up quickly and looks out the window, surveying the parking lot. His hand rests on the door handle. "On the count of ten, we're going to jump out and get in the back seat. One...two...TEN!" Weston's door flies open and rain blows into the cab before I can throw my own door open, but soon we're both in the back seat of my Jeep, wiping the rain from our faces.

"Is this the reason you offered me gum? So I would taste delicious when you finally put the moves on me?" His face is now dangerously close, and I can smell the mint on his breath.

I shrug. "Maybe, maybe not."

"Want to find out?" He digs a piece of scrap paper from his pocket before removing the gum from his mouth and depositing it there.

"Yes," I whisper, and my head falls to the headrest. Weston's face is suddenly inches from mine, and even though it's dark, I can see every line etched in his face. We study each other quietly until his large hand comes up to rest on my face, the only noise from the pounding rain.

I must say, it's incredibly romantic, and if there were ever a perfect scenario a girl could create in her mind, it would be this one—a hundred million times over.

"I've been waiting all day to do this," Weston says, the mint from his breath touching my face before his lips do, soft and light. In the dark of the back seat of my Jeep, his lips linger over the corner of my eyelid, brushing there for the briefest of seconds. "And this…" Now his lips brush the tip of my nose in the barest of touches, so delicately my lips begin to ache.

I inhale the smell of him: his light cologne, the scent of his forest-y shampoo, the fresh aroma of the rain in his hair—and probably mine too. Without thinking, my cheek grazes the side of his face, and I sniff along his strong jawline, wondering where this self-control is coming from. "You smell so good," I murmur.

Then his fingers are running through my ponytail, caressing the long silky strands before he lets it go and plants his hands behind my head, and I know now he's about to kiss me. "I wouldn't mind kissing your lips every day," he says the instant before our lips meet, slowly—almost excruciatingly so—and it's so very different from that urgent first kiss on my front porch. The lightness of this contact has me sighing out loud.

Have you ever kissed someone and you could…feel them *smiling*? Because I swear that's what Weston is doing, and soon I'm grinning too, because honestly, I'm so damn blissful in this moment.

I could live in this car, surviving solely on his kisses.

Weston pulls his head back to look at me. "What are you smiling at?" he asks, holding my face in his hands, stroking my temples with his thumb.

"Same thing you are, I imagine. Why aren't you kissing me?" I pucker my lips, and he does.

Weston

I'll be the first to admit that being in the back seat of this Jeep isn't the most ideal situation, but it beats the hell out of the front, where there were too many obstacles in the way, one being the clutch separating the two front seats.

So even though I'm way too big to be back here, it's more fun than I've had in a long time, and I can't stop myself from smiling, even though we're in the middle of a kiss.

I pull my head back so I can look at Molly directly and ask, "What are you smiling at?"

Her teeth are bright white against her golden skin, and I can see the tiny freckles on her nose even though the only light is from the street lamps in the parking lot, and the heavy sheets of rain are dimming them considerably.

"Same thing you are, I imagine." The smile hasn't left her face, but then she cocks her head sideways and asks, "Why aren't you kissing me?" Molly puckers those wonderfully juicy lips, and, unable to resist, I tip my head forward the smallest inch and suction my mouth to her bottom lip, sucking it and running my tongue along her teeth.

Her mouth opens, and our tongues meet in an all-consuming kiss that leaves us both breathless. It's my favorite kind: sloppy and wet; neither of us care about taking our time. I might even be drooling. Who the hell knows?

Who the hell cares?

Molly's teeth nibble hesitantly at my lower lip and I feel her shiver. I place my hands upon her shoulders, running them up and down her arms before spanning them on her waist, dangerously close to the underside of her breasts. My fingers begin itching to travel south, down to the threadbare hem of her navy-blue tank top, and, never one to ignore my inner urges, I let them do just that.

Her breath hitches and her back arches in an unspoken invitation.

Molly

Oh my god, oh my god, are the only words going through my head right now—well, those and, *Holy shit, he's about to touch my boobs.* As Weston's capable fingers trail the length of my shirt, lightly skimming back and forth along the hem, I bite back the small gasp stuck in my throat, afraid it will make me sound like the virgin I am *not*.

The reality is…I really don't have much experience with guys, and I've only been felt up a handful of times.

It's confession time. I've only ever had sex *one* time.

Here's the ugly truth: I didn't want to head off to college without having done it *at least* once—the world's *worst* logic, I know—and if my parents found out the circumstances, they would be so pissed.

Matt would go postal.

It happened one weekend about four months ago. My whole family was in Madison for one of Matt's hockey games when my parents naïvely let me spend the night at Matt's house instead of with them at their hotel. I wasn't drunk, I wasn't getting out of control, but the opportunity presented itself in the form of hottie Badger goalie Ryan LeShea, who flirted and followed me around all night, and who had *no problem* whatsoever doing the honor of debauching me after a raucous victory party.

It wasn't magical.

It hurt like *hell*.

It definitely *wasn't* love or anything even remotely close to it.

And yeah, I haven't seen him since (not that I want to).

So, as Weston's fingers graze the skin under my thin shirt, I can't help but tense up slightly from the contact and hope he doesn't notice. It feels foreign to have a guy's hand up my shirt, even though it feels *great*. Suddenly he halts his movements. "Is this okay, babe?" he asks. "If you're not comfortable, I can stop." Weston is looking down at me, concern in his dark brown eyes.

It's the word *babe* that does it for me.

I love hearing it, almost as much as I love…

Instead of speaking, I take his hand and guide it higher. He groans into my neck as his fingers skim the underside of my breasts, teasing the light fabric of my bra.

Weston

Molly feels so good I could almost cry.

Okay, so obviously that is an exaggeration, but I'm merely trying to illustrate a point. Touching Molly and kissing her is…beyond amazing.

Her skin is ridiculously soft, and my hands are so calloused and rough that I'm slightly awestruck by the difference. I feel her body tense up when my fingers graze her stomach, so I pull away again to ask, "Is this okay, babe?

If you're not comfortable, I can stop."

The *babe* reference slips out again before I can stop it, but it sounds nice to my ears, and apparently to Molly's, too, because her eyes get big and fill with something that looks to me like adoration. She takes my hand and guides it underneath her shirt.

Then my brain goes to a place it's gone to a million times before, only this time I blurt my thoughts out aloud, well ahead of any common sense, and with no thought to the consequences. I know I shouldn't say it, but I do. "Molly, are you…a virgin?"

Her lips hover over my jawline, and I feel her rapid breathing on my neck. "Why? Are you planning on defiling me tonight?"

"No! I mean…I'd be lying if I said I didn't want to, but no." *Let's see, how do I put this?* "But oh my god, it's all I can think about—not that I'd want to do it in a Jeep…well, yeah, I *would* do it in the Jeep if you—"

Yeah, yeah, I know I'm babbling, but not for long, because Molly cuts my words off, devouring my lips before I can say anything even *more* stupid—hard to believe, right? Her hands rake through my hair, and her fingernails scraping along my scalp feel fucking amazing, almost as good as her lips…but not quite.

We make out like this for who knows how long, until I feel the pressure of Molly's palms against my chest. She pushes at me, shoving my shoulders into the back of the seat until I'm facing forward, and before I can protest the loss of our contact, she surprises me by easing a leg up over my lap to straddle me.

I grab her waist with renewed enthusiasm.

My hands effortlessly find their way back under her shirt, and my crotch gets even harder, if that's even possible. I skim the underside of her bra, brushing my fingers back and forth against the lacy obstacle before my index finger lazily trails upward to trace the edge just above the cup.

I briefly wonder what color her bra is before my palm envelops her entire breast. I feel its weight under my hand and give it a light squeeze, which earns me a throaty moan and a few grinding gyrations from Molly's hips into my groin.

"*Fuck me,* that feels good," I croak out before I can stop myself. "Shit, Molly, don't stop doing that." My plea is desperate, even to my own ears, as her denim-clad ass grinds down on my erection, but it's been months since I've been laid, and even longer since it's been anyone I actually gave a shit about. Okay, to be fair, I've never given a shit about anyone I've ever had sex with, so this whole caring thing is something new, and I plan to enjoy it.

Even in the back seat of a cramped Jeep.

Molly's incredible tits are in my face now, the neckline of her tank top dipping so low from the pull of my hands inside it that her breasts are nearly exposed. As Molly gasps out loud from my ministrations and buries her fingers deeper in the hair atop my head, I lean forward the slightest inch to press my lips against her soft neck, trailing hot kisses down her collarbone, toward her cleavage with a purpose.

Unable to stop myself, I lick between the valley of her breasts, letting my hot tongue linger on her salty skin. She smells like citrus, an aroma I've come to fully appreciate as being uniquely Molly. I can't even eat an orange in the school cafeteria these days without getting turned on, for God's sake.

Somewhere from inside the Jeep, a cell phone rings.

Caught up in each other, we ignore it.

"Oh, Weston, yeah," Molly mutters. So sexy.

The phone begins ringing again, and through my fuzzy, sex-crazed haze, I recognize the ringtone. It's my mom.

Fuck shit, double shit.

"Babe, I have to get that," I gasp into Molly's plump cleavage. "It's my mom. She'll kill me if I don't answer it." Groaning, Molly untangles herself from my lap, and I let my palm cup her ass before it lands in the seat next to mine.

Digging in my pants pocket, I extract my cell and make quick work of redialing my parents. Immediately, my mom's voice answers. "Where are you? It's raining buckets, and your father was just about to come out looking for you."

"I'm stranded in a parking lot, waiting it out with a friend."

Brief pause.

My mom's not an idiot. "Does this *friend* have a vehicle that can deliver you home? You can leave the bike and your dad can bring you back to get it later."

I glance at Molly. "Yes."

"Okay. Then she can come in and meet us when you get here. I expect you home in fifteen minutes."

Click.

The line goes dead, and I stare at my phone.

"What did she say?" Molly asks from beside me with wide eyes, cheeks flushed from my five o'clock shadow and lips swollen from my kisses.

Unable to resist the temptation, I lean over and give her an open-mouth kiss before saying, "They want to meet you."

Molly

Dear Lord, did he just say what I think he said?

"They want to…meet me?" Stupidly I repeat what he just told me, which, incidentally, I absolutely hate when people do to me. Drives me *bonkers*.

"Yeah. I mean, I don't think that was originally the intention, but now that I'm stranded here, the opportunity presented itself. My mom said they want me to leave the bike here and when you bring me home, they want you to come in and meet them. Are you cool with that?" Weston looks at me expectantly.

"I… *Sure*. I mean…I guess the better question here is, are *you* okay with it?"

He opens his mouth to answer, but before any words come out, there is a loud banging on the back window. We both turn in surprise to see Mary and Olivia with their hands and faces pressed up against the glass, and now they're shouting, but I can't for the life of me understand what they're saying.

"What the fuck?" Weston voices exactly what I'm thinking before scooting over and rolling the window down halfway, rain suddenly intruding on our warm, dry haven. "What the hell are you two doing?" he asks, completely disgusted.

"Mary was worried you were stranded because your crotch rocket is still here, so we wanted to check and see if you needed a ride." The rain is battering down on them both, and now they look like drowned rats. At this point, Olivia's mascara is running down her face, and she looks like Alice Cooper, a rock star from the eighties who resembles a corpse—or a zombie, whatever it is you're into.

"Are you fucking *kidding* me? I'm in the back of a Jeep with my…with Molly. Why would you think I needed a ride home?"

Okay, even I'll admit he's being a tad harsh.

Olivia and Mary just stand in the dark parking lot, rain shining under the dull street lamps that fail to light it. Water drips off Mary's nose as she stands there getting soaked, and I can't help but take pity on them. "Go, you guys! Go dry off before you get sick. We're leaving anyway."

They turn and run through the parking lot toward their beat-up red car, and Weston rolls up the back window. "Can you believe that? Not a lick of common sense between them."

"Well…one of them has a crush on you, so I'm sure they thought they were being helpful." Why I'm defending them when they so clearly ignored me twice today is beyond me, but it truly is hard *not* to feel somewhat sorry for someone begging for attention from a guy as good-looking and popular as Weston McGrath. It's almost unavoidable.

What can I say? He has a way about him that makes girls crazy.

Not *me,* obviously, but…lots of girls.

"Maybe so, but that was annoying." He looks at me

and runs his fingers through his hair. "I guess we can't sit here feeling each other up all night, as much as I'd like to, so let's get cranking and get this meeting with my parents over with."

23

Weston

"Give me a little credit for intelligence, would you, son? I could eat a can of alphabet soup and shit out a better excuse than the one you just gave me." – Brian McGrath

I wouldn't say my palms are sweaty as we walk into my house—I mean, it could be the rain making my hands wet—but I swipe them over my jeans to dry them anyway then guide Molly into the laundry room from the garage. I can hear my mom in the kitchen and a few other noises that sound like dishes being put away.

I glance down at the top of Molly's head, barely resisting the urge to plant a kiss on the bow of her ponytail in a show of support, and brace myself as we enter the kitchen. Immediately I spot Kendall, who is sitting at the island, shoulders bent over a notebook, markers spread out in front of her. She glances up when we walk through the doorframe, her face registering surprise as she spots Molly, then her stare turns to curiosity as her eyebrows shoot up.

She cocks her head and studies Molly with open fascination. "Who is that?" Kendall all but points, setting down her marker. The question floats across the kitchen, drawing attention to us.

Great, just what I need, my little sister gawking at Molly like she's never seen a girl before. Okay, let me clarify: like she's never seen a girl I've brought *home* before.

All right, let me clarify *again*: like she's never seen a girl I've brought home whom I've had good intentions toward. I've definitely brought girls to the house, just not usually with the intention of conversing with my family, if you catch my drift.

My mom turns, and I can already see the grin forming on her face as she walks toward us, wiping her hands on a dish towel. Her arms are already extended, and as she's reaching for Molly, I notice how much shorter she is. Then I think, *Crap, my mom's going in for a hug.*

This is going to be nightmare.

But instead of recoiling, which is what any other girl would have done, Molly leans in for my mom's hug like it's no big deal, emitting a low, content laugh. "Hello, Mrs. McGrath. It's nice to meet you. It smells good in here. Did you just have dinner?"

I let out the breath I'm holding.

"Yup, just cleaning up and loading the dishwasher. And please, call me Laura. We had pot roast, Weston. Shame on your for not bringing Molly home to eat with us! Just look at you both; you're soaking wet," my mom exclaims, turning to my sister. "Kendall, go get some towels, sweetie, for your brother and his friend." She turns and looks at us again—actually, she's only looking at Molly—still smiling. She just can't wipe it off her face, it seems.

Must be a mom thing.

Kendall slowly inches off the barstool. In fact, she's so slow that if I were on fire and needed her to grab an extinguisher, I would be *dead* by now. She's got this shit-eating grin on her face as she says, "By friend, do you really mean *girlfriend*? Because I heard mom talking about you on the phone the other day, and that's what she called you." The little brat actually used air quotes with her fingers when she said *friend*.

Holy shit. "Jesus, Kendall, what the hell!"

Kendall shrugs innocently. "What? It's a legitimate question."

"Weston Richard, watch your mouth! And Kendall Rebecca McGrath, stop embarrassing your brother and go get him and Molly each a towel. Now!" My mom follows her out of the room, probably to lecture her more about embarrassing me—that itself is horrifying—and to make sure the smart-ass little shit is actually going to fetch some dry towels.

And…it's back to being a complete nightmare. I can feel the color rising up my neck, and my face is scorching hot. I don't even want to glance over at Molly, but I can feel her shoulders shaking next to me and can hear short sputters of what sounds like a muffled laugh.

"You think that's funny?" I ask her indignantly, crossing my arms over my chest.

"Oh Weston, you should *see* your face. Priceless." Her gaze flickers over my biceps, lazily over my forearms, and she bites down on her lower lip. "You look so…*cute* right now, all flustered and blushing." she whispers, her green eyes shining, almost like she's stripping me naked in her mind and liking what she sees.

I groan. "You can't say shit like that in my parent's kitchen. Now I want to tackle you to the ground."

"Maybe I think it's fun to tease you," she sasses me.

I'm about to reach for her when my dad makes his appearance.

"Well, look who finally made it home in one piece. Looks like you two got stuck in the rain." My dad walks into the kitchen wearing jeans and a Ravens fleece, his big frame filling the entire doorway. He walks to the counter and, with his back to us, lifts the coffee carafe out of the coffee maker, gets a mug out of the cabinet, and proceeds to pour himself a cup while we stand there idly.

I take him in, trying to picture what Molly sees.

It's not uncommon for people to be intimidated by him. Shit, even I am occasionally.

Finally, my dad turns and faces us, slowly stirring his drink before tapping the coffee mug with the spoon and setting it in the sink. He eyes Molly critically, one eyebrow crooked, at the same time his giant hand reaches out for a shake. "Brian McGrath. You must be Molly. Can't say we've heard all that much about you." He says this nonchalantly and sips his coffee, watching us over the brim of the mug for our reaction.

What an ass.

"Brian!" my mom admonishes, her soft features flush, and she turns a dark shade of pink as she reenters the kitchen. "What he *means* is we're so glad to finally meet you. By chance, I noticed you at the last home game."

I want to say, *Yeah, everyone noticed because I couldn't stop myself from eye fucking her from the ice*, but I hold my tongue. Molly and I aren't touching, and I find myself wanting to reach for her hand. It's not necessarily to protect her from my parents—well, mostly just my dad, because my mom's being way cooler than I thought she would be—but to make it easier on her.

Molly's face flushes with a little blush of her own. "Oh, well. That wasn't my choice; I was coerced into going." She elbows me shyly in the ribs, and my dad's steely gaze bores holes into her, like he can't believe she'd touch me in front of him.

My dad sets down the coffee mug and crosses his arms, leaning against the granite countertop. "And how does that work? Being coerced into going?"

What is this, the Spanish Inquisition?

So, I might as well tell you this: my dad doesn't want me dating.

Ever.

It's like I mentioned before, he wants me to focus solely on hockey, which I've always done. An occasional lay on the side is fine, as long as it doesn't interfere with my game and he doesn't have to see or hear about it. You know what they say: out of sight, out of mind.

Having someone steady or an actual girlfriend?

Not on the list of priorities he's made for me.

So, yeah. It's obvious that he's not pleased, and he's acting like someone pissed in his Cheerios.

Suddenly, the gender roles are reversed, and Molly has become the proverbial guy every dad dreads and waits for on their front porch while polishing their shotguns. Thankfully, my mom crosses the room and lays her hand on my dad's arm. I consider this his warning. Mom is the only person who can calm my dad the fuck down.

"Would you kids like to sit? Let's go into the living room."

We follow my parents into the living room, and much to my horror, Kendall is perched on the end of the couch with her giant, fat tabby cat Jazzy in her lap, and instead of tuning in to the television, she's watching us with a smirk on her face.

For an eleven-year-old, she acts like a nosey teenager, and up until right this second, it's never really bothered me. At *this* particular moment, she is *bugging* the living *shit* out of me.

Even her damn cat seems like a cocky little asshole.

My mom motions for us to sit on the couch. Just to be on the safe side, I sit directly next to Kendall. I have a feeling she's going to be like a loose cannon, and those lips aren't going to stay closed for very long. Eventually she's going to want to get her two cents in.

Warily, I watch her from the corner of my eye as Dad sits directly across from us in his favorite leather chair. Leaning forward, he clasps his hands in front of him and props his elbow on his knees. I can hear him thinking from across the room.

My mom clears her throat and plasters her trademark optimistic smile on her face.

Could this be any more awkward?

24

Molly

"Awkward? That's an understatement." – Molly

Can someone tell me again why I'm here?

Mr. McGrath, with his big brooding stare, is watching me from his seat—a big leather La-Z-Boy recliner that looks like it has seen better days. I would even bet money that Weston's mom has tried to toss it to the curb a few times.

It looks like Mrs. McGrath—Laura—is about to say something, but Kendall interrupts.

"So, Molly, what grade are you in? Are you a senior too?" She sits innocently, watching me with big doe eyes, her hand lazily stroking the orange cat that's sleeping on her lap.

"Yes, I'm a senior too. How about you? What grade are you in, Kendall?"

She perks up with importance. "I'm in middle school this year," she says, flipping her hair over her shoulder. "Sixth grade. Did you have Mrs. Deerfield for any classes when you were my age?"

"You know, I think I did! She was one of my favorites." I smile shyly as Kendall nods her head enthusiastically.

"Her class is my favorite, but I have this kid, Ben, who sits behind me, and he's always pulling my hair. Last week I finally told him if he didn't stop, my brother would jam a hockey stick so far up his ass he wouldn't walk for a week."

To illustrate her point, Kendall takes her fist and pretends to jam it in the air.

"Kendall!" Weston's mom shrieks loudly, her horrified voice vibrating through the cavernous family room. "*What* did I tell you about using that word? Where on *Earth* did you learn to say things like that?"

Slowly, all our eyes move to Weston, who is suddenly fidgeting in his seat. He curls his lips in a scowl and throws his hands up. "Fine! It was me! *Someone* needed to teach her to defend herself!"

Mrs. McGrath is bright red. "That is *not* teaching her how to defend herself, young man. That's threatening another person with bodily harm—and a child no less! Telling your sister you'll shove a hockey stick up someone's bum, indeed!"

"Bum," Kendall mutters sassily, breaking the awkward silence that followed Mrs. McGraths shocked outburst. "So, Molly, is my brother as cool at school as he thinks he is?"

"Mom, please make her stop."

"Come on, I need to know! He walks around here like he owns the place. I'm not even allowed in his *room* without permission," Kendall huffs with a pout.

"Well, no kidding. The last time you went in there you let Jazzy sleep in my sock drawer while you used all my printer paper to make snowflakes. There were tiny scraps of paper everywhere for weeks."

"Pfft, big deal. It's not like I was in there reading that journal you keep under your mattress."

"Oh my god, Kendall, I swear to all that is holy—"

Mr. McGrath, God bless him, clears his throat for the millionth time, and I might be mistaken, but there is a laugh threatening to burst out of him. "All right, guys, that's enough," he finally says, the low baritone of his voice silencing everyone else in the room. He gives Kendall a warning look then shakes his head at Weston before directing his gaze at me. "So. Molly." He pauses. "Matthew Wakefield is your brother, huh?"

Once again, he clasps his hands in front of him and leans forward in his chair. Weston quietly groans beside me and nudges my knee with his thigh. "Dad…" he warns.

I put my hand on his knee but snatch it back immediately, for Mr. McGrath's eyes follow my movement and narrow. I receive the message loud and clear: *no touching.*

Got it.

"Yes, sir. He's finishing his last year at Madison, and he's been drafted."

"Do you suppose that's what my son sees in you?"

Weston shouts, "Dad!" at the same time Mrs. McGrath shouts, "Brian!"

If I had been drinking liquid at the moment, I'm fairly certain I would have spit it out.

"It's a fair question, I would think. Weston is a senior and has never had an interest in girls, because he's focused on his *hockey* career, then suddenly he's 'dating' the sister of a future Anaheim Duck? Am I the only one who's not seeing what's wrong with this picture?"

He scratches his chin as if in deep thought.

What a jerk.

Laura McGrath stands abruptly, marches over to her husband, and says through clenched teeth, "Brian, sweetheart, can I see you in the kitchen, please?" Not waiting for a response, she jerks him up by his arm and stalks out of the living room, towing him behind.

"Sheesh, this just got awk…*ward*," Kendall muses. "Bet Molly's gonna think twice about coming back over here, eh Weston."

"Shut *up*, Kendall," Weston grits out, his face contorted into a look of disgust. "Come on, Molly, let's go get my bike." He hauls me up and turns to his sister, ruffling the top of her head affectionately with his fingers. "Tell Mom I'll be back in an hour."

Weston

Kendall was right. That was freaking awkward.

What the fuck was my dad's deal?

We ride in silence for a few miles in Molly's Jeep—she let me drive—the rain still coming down, but in a gentle rhythm, more of a delicate mist than a heavy downpour; it would be soothing if not for the circumstances surrounding us like a cloud.

I honestly have no idea what to say. "Molly…" is all that comes out. If she were one of my guy friends, I would demand that she shrug it off because my dad is nothing but an overgrown prick and a bully, but she's *not* one of my guy friends.

She's…

Different. I want to say special, but that sounds douchey, and sappy, and we've already established that I'm neither.

"It's okay. You don't have to say anything," Molly says softly next to me, and now I feel like an even bigger ass. I don't like it, but the reality is, I'm not going to waltz into my parent's kitchen and tell my dad off to defend her. He would have kicked my ass.

"I know, but…" My eyes are trained on the road, and I'm trying my damndest to focus on our conversation, but the combination of wet road and the glare from the street lights makes it hard to find the yellow line in the middle of the road. I don't want to get us in an accident.

Molly takes a deep breath. "Listen, Weston…that totally sucked back there, and I'd be lying if I said I wasn't going to take it personally"—another deep breath—"but don't think for one second that I haven't witnessed that scene before, or some version of it. I mean, Matthew is my brother, and he had girls falling all over him for all the wrong reasons. Still does." Her head is down, and she's fiddling with the zipper pull on her jacket. "Your parents just don't want some gold digger to get their claws into you because they think you're going to be playing pro someday—or worse, for you to get some sleaze pregnant, no matter who her brother is, so…yeah. I get it."

"I know you're not a gold digger, Molly, and to be honest...I wish you were a bigger sleaze."

Shocked, but probably not as much as she's acting like she is, Molly gapes at me with her mouth hanging open, and we both burst out laughing.

"I feel bad for my mom. My dad is so out of control with the whole hockey thing. Did you see how pissed she was? He's probably *still* getting his ass chewed out."

I clutch the wheel out of frustration.

"Yeah, I think she felt bad for me more than anything," Molly says, a wide grin illuminating her face. "That sister of yours is a little stinker."

"You think? Dude, you have no idea how many times that kid has embarrassed the shit out of me. She's a beast."

"Oh yeah? How so?"

I cock my head in thought, trying to come up with a really good Kendall story. "Ah, I've got one. For starters, last year my parents dropped me off at a hockey clinic in Cleveland—are you picturing this? When we got to the ice rink, there were *all* these coaches standing around outside the locker room. Instead of keeping her mouth shut like a normal ten-year-old, Kendall walks up to Jeremy Hartman from Philly and says in this snotty voice, 'Just so you know, my brother here says you suck and he's going to totally whoop your guys' butts.' If my mom hadn't grabbed her and clamped her hand over Kendall's mouth, she would have kept talking. That was the world's shittiest week. I got checked into the boards every time someone from Philly skated by. Bruised for weeks afterward."

"No!" Molly gasps.

"Yeah. And don't think for one second that kid didn't

know those guys were going to be after me. She isn't an idiot."

"Maybe she's around too many hockey players." Molly laughs, resting her damp hair against the back of the seat, her neck thrown back and exposed. Like a moth to a flame, I look and have the urge to pull the Jeep over just so I can run my fingers across the smooth skin of her cheek. Instead, I clear my throat and focus on the road.

I'm not even going to try examining my feelings for her right now.

Too complicated.

25

Molly

"It just keeps getting better and better, doesn't it?" – Jenna

As hard as I tried, last night I could not lose the image of Weston's dad in my head—the image of him leaning forward to glare at me like I was the devil's spawn out to corrupt his son.

His golden child.

For the first time in a few weeks, I'm very confused. Instead of the fluttery butterflies that once resided in my stomach, I've had a knot transplanted there.

I can see Jenna in the lunch line, bouncing on her heels as she retells a story—or at least, I'm going to assume that's what she's doing—to Olivia Wilder. I'm not alone at our lunch table, but I definitely feel like an island with so much weight on my shoulders.

Hurry, hurry, hurry, I chant inside my head.

Ugh, so much to tell her, and she's either going to freak out on me or have a good dose of advice. I'm hoping it's the latter.

Eventually, Jenna weaves her way through the crowded cafeteria and plops down next to me, the light, fluttery breeze kicking up the soft smell of her flowery perfume. I take a little whiff and lean over. "You smell good," I say, giving her a little wink and nudging her with my leg. "What's the occasion?"

"Always look and smell your best, that's my motto," she jokes, grabbing a petite carrot off her tray and popping it into her mouth with a crunch. "So, since you never called me last night, I'm going to assume the absolute best case scenario—that you were ravished in the back of your car and no longer have to live with the memory of giving your V-card to some drunk college dude. Please, dear god, tell me that's what happened."

This loud declaration earns me a few stares from our other friends at the table, and I kick Jenna under the table. Why is she always—and I do mean *always*—so damn obnoxious?

"Okay, loud mouth, first of all, he was not *drunk*," I hiss, even though I'm lying, but Jenna holds her hand up to silence me.

"Can we skip all the idle chit-chat and get to the good stuff? According to my Swatch watch, we have thirty-two minutes. Time is of the essence. Just tell me this: Did. He. Touch. Your. Boobs?" *Crunch crunch* go more carrots, which, now that I'm looking at her, match the chevron shirt she's got on. She looks adorable today with her hair in a messy bun and large hoop earrings swaying from her ears.

Damn her for being so perky and cute.

"Do you know how hard it is for me to sit here and not smack you?" Now, only a few people are staring, so I give my best fake smile, let out a low fake laugh, and mutter through clenched teeth, "If you don't knock it off, I'm not telling you a damn thing. Do you think I want Stacy to hear all my personal business?"

Stacy Bingham is my only frienemy. She always sits at our table, and although I have no real reason to dislike her, we have just never gotten along like good friends do. There's always just been something about her I don't trust…and now she's watching me over her brown paper lunch sack, keenly aware something is going on at the other side of the table.

Stacy squints at us.

"Sorry. Please forgive me, and do proceed."

Glancing around the lunchroom, I haven't been able to get a visual of Weston. He has yet to make an appearance in the cafeteria, and it's distracting me. I can't stop myself from craning my neck to check out the jock table every couple of minutes.

I start my story. "So, yesterday after he went to practice and I told Alexis Peterson to kiss our asses, we went to Kyoto. That was fine. All we did was chat and eat. Well, okay, we did get into an argument because I think he's kind of stringing me along. Not on purpose, just…he doesn't have time to date, you know? Anyway, I walked out on him and he chased me into the rain."

"Oh em gee, like in *The Notebook*?" Jenna squeaks.

"Huh? No, Jenna, *not* like in *The Notebook*. Not at all. Where do you come up with this? Ugh, anyway, he runs out of the restaurant and we climb into my Jeep, because at this point, it's pouring rain."

"Did you fog up the glass? Eh, eh?" Now my best friend is winking at me, but instead of being sly, she's coming off as incredibly pervy, and then she gives me a onceover. "You look super cute today, by the way. Why haven't I seen that shirt? I totally dug through your entire closet Saturday night."

I glance down at my top. She's right, it is super cute. It's an aqua-blue lace shirt that hangs slightly off my shoulders, and underneath it is a blue tank top. Paired with skinny jeans and brown equestrian boots, it's definitely one of my better days.

Suddenly I'm feeling warm and fuzzy and decide to be generous. "Yeah, we totally made out in the back of my car. It was amazing…"

"Yes! I knew it! I'm not even going to ask if it was any good because I can tell just by the dreamy look on your face that it was. Nice." Jenna takes a bite of her turkey sandwich and chews for a little bit before asking, "So, he felt you up, and then…?"

"Well, this is where it got weird. His parents called and wanted to meet me, but his dad was…not pleased. You know, he thinks I'm…" I struggle to find the right words to describe the moment.

"A homewrecker? A slut? Vixen. Trampy." I stare holes into Jenna, giving her the *are you done yet* glare, but she doesn't take the hint. "A hoe-bag. A floozy. He thinks you're one of *those girls,* doesn't he?"

"Jenna, stop." At this point I'm laughing because really, is there any better way to react? She's cracking me up.

The other girls at the table are openly curious, but they

know better than to ask us what's so funny. As much as I hate to admit it, Jenna, Tasha, Maddie, and I are a tight clique that's almost impossible to penetrate.

"Oh shit, there he is. *Damn,* he's good lookin'," Jenna says as she bites into a Hostess cupcake. She shoves the last piece in her mouth in one large chunk then makes a production out of moaning and groaning. "Mmmm, oh yeah, baby, this is good."

My fork pauses halfway to my mouth, and I roll my eyes. Okay, I'm kind of amused.

Kind of.

"Any day now…" I mutter, tapping my fingers on the table with a small smile on my face as I wait patiently for her to stop showboating with her cupcake. Such a guy thing to do.

"Okay, but honestly, Molly, he's so hot. Light your pants on fire, hold on to your daughters, H-O-T *hot.*" Jenna takes the hem of her shirt and fans it, letting the cool cafeteria air graze her skin.

"Jeez, Jenna, don't you think it's a little rude to be talking about someone's…your friend's…" I wave my hand around in the air, searching for a word that's not *boyfriend.* "Your friend's *whatever he is* like he's a piece of meat?"

Jenna gets quiet, and she gives me a look I've seen a million times—the one that says, *What the hell are you babbling about, because I am not amused.* With her eyebrow cocked and lip pulled up into a tight purse, kind of like that Olympic gymnast…what's her name…McKayla Maroney.

That face.

Then she says, "Are you kidding me? You're going to

deny me the opportunity to ogle? I'm dating Alex Mitchell, for crying out loud, who I'm pretty sure has a pocket protector stashed in his sock drawer. So no, you don't get to comment on my harmless infatuation. In fact, you kind of owe me in a way…"

"*What!* How do I owe you?" I am practically screeching—not a good look for me, as I'm pretty sure my face and chest are beet red.

"How *don't* you? Are you freaking kidding me? You haven't dated anyone in, well, *ever*, and as your best friend"—her eyes dart around the table and she gives everyone knowing glances, like a queen addressing her public—"as your *best* friend, all I ever do is sit and tell you about my fantastic love life"—I raise my eyebrow at this proclamation—"and you never have anything to tell me about yours! So yeah, you owe me. It's been seventeen years in the making, doll face, so get used to it."

Doll face?

"I'm not saying I don't want to tell you what's going on. I'm saying could you please stop undressing him with your eyes and making sex noises while you eat cupcakes? That's what I'm saying."

"Oh. Well, okay, sure. I can do that," she says, patting my hand while she glances over my shoulder. Then she pouts as she adds, "He's not even looking over here."

"Of all the nerve," I sarcastically reply, biting into the pizza on my tray. Most students don't exactly enjoy school cafeteria food, but I will tell you this: I am not most people, and school pizza happens to be my favorite, with the grilled cheese and tomato soup coming in at a close second. Unable to resist, I lean into Jenna and ask, "What's he doing now?"

She looks over, earrings swaying airily. "He's..." She sits up straighter to get a better look over the sea of heads. "He's eating...and"—she strains her neck up and squints—"he looks angry, but then again, what else is new?" Jenna flops back down in her seat. "That's a look I like to call sexy angry." She points at me with her index finger. "You better get on that."

"Get your finger out of my face." I laugh, smacking her hand away and taking a sip of my bottled water. Unable to stop myself, I chew my bottom lip and glance in Weston's general direction in the cafeteria, even though I can't see him above the fray.

"Have you talked to him at all today?"

"No. We only have study hall together. He's not exactly..." I pause and play with the cap on the plastic bottle in my hands.

Jenna leans in and quietly says, "Generous with outward affection?"

Surprised, I glance up at her with a wry smile on my face, glad she kind of gets it without me having to explain. This relationship isn't exactly what I'd call *complicated*, but it's not exactly a walk in the park either. I mean, because he has something of an obligation to his sport, I haven't been made to feel like any kind of priority.

And until this moment, I guess I didn't realize how bad that felt.

Feeling a bit bummed, I nod my head and fake a smile.

Weston

26

"Dude, you're dating my ex-girlfriend? I'm eating a sandwich. Did you want some of those leftovers too?" – more wit from cousin Jake

*Y*ou'll have to take my word for it when I say it's damn hard to eat a decent lunch when you're surrounded by idiots. Not only is it loud in this godforsaken place, but also the guys at my table—my "friends"—don't make it any better by competing to be the most obnoxious and immature.

We have a game this weekend, and although it's four days away, I am trying to get my head in the game. Instead, I'm being mind-fucked by the memory of my dad's attitude toward Molly and her reaction to it.

Seriously, I don't have time for shit like that, and it just goes to prove that is the exact reason I don't get involved with the opposite sex. Even though, to be fair, the drama wasn't created by Molly—but it did happen *because* of her.

Keeping my head down to ignore the crude remarks buzzing around the table, I pull my ball cap farther down over my eyes and hunch my shoulders to lean over my tray. I'm sure I look like Quasimodo from *The Hunchback of Notre Dame*, but I don't give a shit.

I have a lot on mind and I'm still hungry, even after one banana, two slices of greasy pizza, three Otis Spunkmeyer cookies, and one Mountain Dew. My eyes scan the trays of my friends in front of me, and I notice Bryan Bossner has half a hamburger on his tray.

Without asking, I reach for it.

"What the hell, man!" Despite his protests, I cram it into my mouth, shoving it all in in one piece.

"I'm hungry," I mumble with a mouthful, barely able to get the words out.

"How is that my problem? I wasn't done with that, asshole. Get your lazy ass up and go buy yourself something."

Irritated, I shoot him a look, finish chewing, then swallow before saying, "Don't fucking call me lazy."

Bryan tries to stare me down, and it looks like he wants to tell me to go fuck myself, but a few seconds later he looks away instead. For the briefest of seconds, I feel a small stab of guilt, if you can call it that, but when I glance down the table and catch Rick watching me from the corner of his eye, the feeling disappears.

If anyone can make me lose my shit, it's him.

To be fair, I haven't heard much from him since I threatened to kick his ass, and I know he hasn't spoken to Molly either, but still, I don't trust him, and I sure as hell don't like him, even if I have to call him teammate.

A few minutes later, when I've dumped my garbage

and stored my lunch tray on the tall kitchen cart, I make my way down the somewhat empty hallway toward my locker. Since mostly everyone is either in class or in the cafeteria, it's quiet and I don't have to think about anything but my locker combination as I stand there dialing it.

I stand at my locker, trying to clear all the bullshit from my mind, when that stream of peaceful nothingness is interrupted by a loud, insistent clearing of a delicate throat. Expecting to see Molly when I lift my head, a smile spreads to my face.

And then quickly disappears.

"Hey, Weston. So, you haven't called me lately."

Shit.

Stacy Bingham stands next to my locker, brown eyes fluttering, lips glossed to a sticky shine.

I suddenly wonder if I could escape by squeezing inside my locker. Once, when I was in third grade, we had this complete asshole of a teacher who would make us all climb inside our cubbies when we misbehaved, and this one fat kid, Jameson, got stuck because he never fit inside to begin with.

"Weston, did you hear what I just said?"

I sigh loudly. "Why do you suppose it is that I haven't called, Stacy? How long ago was it that we went out? Five, six months?"

Stacy chews on her thumbnail and appears to be thinking of an answer. She counts out the months on her fingers—no lie. "Um, maybe five?"

"Right...so don't you think I would have *called* if I was interested?"

"Um, I just assumed you were busy and that you didn't have time?"

Okay, this is just downright pathetic. "Stacy, have you ever heard of the book, *He's Just Not That Into You*? Maybe you should download it onto your eReader." I collect the books I need for my next class and stand with my back to the metal door.

"I haven't read the book, but I've seen the movie," she says hopefully, shifting the books in her arms, as if having seen the damn movie was scoring her brownie points or something. I seriously wonder if she's as ignorant as she's making herself look. "The ending is the best, where Gigi and Alex *finally* get together."

What the fuck is she talking about? "Sorry, haven't seen the movie."

"Oh em gee, it's so good. There are these four friends who—"

I cut her off. "And I don't ever want to. So besides coming over here to irritate me, was there anything else? We hooked up at one party in a coatroom, which doesn't exactly classify us as anything."

Stacy's face falls, and she bites her lower lip, which immediately makes me think of Molly, because she does the same thing—only when she does it, it's endearing and irresistible.

"Well, yeah, but I was kind of hoping…." Her voice trails off, just as something occurs to me.

"Stacy, aren't you and Molly Wakefield friends?"

She hesitates. "Um. Kind of, but not really."

"Kind of, but not really?" I mock her in my best nasally girl voice. "What the hell does that even mean? Oh wait, is that code for *I'm a two-faced bitch who sneaks around behind my friends' backs*? Because you probably already know Molly and I have been going out lately."

No longer being able to remain stoic, Stacy snorts. "Yeah, but everyone knows you're not even taking her to Fall Formal."

Now I'm confused. "What does that have to do with anything?"

"Do I have to spell it out for you? *Fine*. If you liked her, you would be taking her to the dance, not ditching her during the biggest social event of the year."

I'm still confused. "So? It's just a damn dance. I have shit to do that night."

"More important shit, apparently," Stacy says smugly, a satisfied mask of expression covering her features. "Are you her boyfriend or not?"

"What? No. How many bloody times do I have to tell you people? Molly Wakefield is not, nor will she ever be, my damn girlfriend."

It's at that same moment that Mr. Pembroke, one of the science teachers, sticks his head out of his classroom and squints down the hallway at us. Clearly, he's not wearing his contacts today. "Oh, Mr. McGrath, it's you." He looks me up and down. "Please keep the cursing and the noise level to a *min*-eh-mum."

It's also the moment Stacy's eyes get wide, and she looks over my shoulder, her cool mask transforming into one of pure glee.

Don't turn around, don't turn around, don't turn around, I chant to myself, because I know exactly who I'm going to see standing there when I do.

27

Molly

"Sometimes your knight in shining armor is really just a douchebag in tin foil." – Jenna, who saw it on the internet

Oh my god, how utterly cliché and predictable could this scene be? No better than an after school special or a Lifetime movie, I stand there in the hall, crushed by the misfortune of having to overhear such spiteful and insensitive words coming out of Weston's mouth.

It's always back to square one with this guy! What the hell? This is, after all, not the first time he's done this to me. Crap, maybe I'm the one who should be reading *He's Just Not That Into You*, because apparently Weston's not as into me as I originally thought.

And just when I thought I might be falling in love with him.

Crash and burn is more like it, because it looks like the joke is on me.

My first impulse, of course, is to flee and get my butt out of the hallway, remove myself entirely from the whole awkward situation.

But I don't.

Hell to the *no*.

I'm stronger than that.

So I do what any self-respecting girl would do: I stand there and confront the situation, watching Stacy Bingham's victorious face over Weston's shoulder. I want that bastard to turn his broad frame to face me, want him to look me in the eyes so he can see the hurt his careless words have caused me.

Again.

He turns, and a few moments pass as he and I just watch each other. I feel a hand on my shoulder, the comforting pull of my best friend slowly tugging me away. She moves to stand in front of me, her small frame a sizzling ball of energy as she stares Stacy down.

Jenna is beyond pissed, and for once, I don't stop her from what she's about to say.

"What the *H* do you think you're doing, Stacy? Haven't you ever heard of girl code? You don't go after your friend's boyfriend."

Stacy laughs. "Oh, but didn't you hear? She's nothing to him, a *nobody*, and most certainly not his girlfriend—right, Weston? Isn't that what you were just telling me?"

That bitch.

Why? *Why* are girls so cruel, I ask you? Just minutes ago we were all sitting at the same lunch table together, laughing—okay, so mostly just Jenna and I were laughing—and talking about what dresses everyone was wearing to the big dance. Even though I'm not going, I was still excited to hear what everyone's plans are.

And Weston, that big lummox of an idiot, just stands there trying to come up with something to say. Now, I'll be the first to admit he was doing pretty well there for a little bit, fending off Stacy's subtle advances by being a complete dick, but here's what I don't understand: why did he get all weird and defensive when she asked if I was his girlfriend? It's like, what the hell, dude—get over it! She was just asking a question. We're not getting married tomorrow for Pete's sake. We just went on a one date and we've been flirting for a few weeks.

Big deal.

Immediately, I'm glad to be female. How terrible would it be not to have any rational thoughts going through that thick head? I swear to you, it's taken every ounce of self-control that I have not to whip out my cell phone and text my brother so he can come beat the crap out of Weston for embarrassing me like this.

I dig deep within myself to force out a laugh, but it comes out low and broken, which is exactly how I feel. Borrowing one of Jenna's favorite words, I mockingly taunt, "Duh, Stacy. Do you think I want to be tied down by a guy who has no life other than hockey? Please, even I'm not that desperate."

Apparently, that's not enough for Jenna, and she nudges me with her elbow. When I don't take her cue, she steps forward dramatically. "You asshole! You big, dumb asshole. I trusted you!"

Dear Lord. Seriously, Jenna?

"Who the hell do you think you are, Weston McGrath, huh? Standing there, looking all hot—er, I mean, not giving a shit about Molly's feelings. Well, let me tell you something, *pal*, you are the one losing out here. And Stacy, if you're gonna be two-faced, at least make sure one of them is pretty."

The whole time Jenna is ranting on, I want to both laugh and cry at the same time. My eyes are locked on Weston's, and I look for any sign that he regrets his words or is going to rescind them.

"Jenna, stop," I say, putting my hand on her arm, because she's acting like a dog with rabies—either that or she's trying to win an Academy Award for Best Dramatic Scene. Because we have an audience, Weston hasn't moved a muscle, and I shake my head gently before saying, "You know, all those times you stand up to people—those jerks you call your friends—now you won't stand and put up a little fight for *me*? The worst part is, I really thought we were friends."

Then, to really drive my point home and to piss him off, I add, "Looks like my brother was right about you."

I turn just in time to see his eyes flash and his nostrils flare as he stares after me.

He's either pissed off or turned on, and all I can think is, *Good*.

But I still want to vomit.

Weston

Yes.

Yes, I am a fucking idiot for letting her walk off. Are you satisfied?

As Molly walks away, her small sassy friend in tow, Stacy sighs beside me and crosses both arms over her flat chest. "Well, that was only *slightly* awkward."

"Why are you still standing here?" I ask rudely, grabbing my books and slamming my locker shut. "If I were you, I would walk away before I do something we're both going to regret."

I start walking toward the math wing.

Undaunted and stepping in line with my brisk pace, Stacy is not taking the hint and lets out a short little laugh. "You're not blaming me for your fuck-up back there, are you? Ugh, such a typical guy thing to do. That scene back there"—she gestures over her shoulder—"that was entirely *your* fault."

I stop dead in my tracks and grab her by the arm. "What the hell is that supposed to mean? If you hadn't pissed me off and pushed all my buttons, I wouldn't have lost my temper."

Her eyebrow shoots up. Slowly she says, "So…let me get this straight. I ask you if Molly's your girlfriend….and because I've already pissed you off, you get mad and yell that she'll never be your—oh wait, how exactly did you put it? She'll never be your 'damn girlfriend.' Do I have it right?"

"Jesus Christ, you're a pain in the ass." I can feel my temper rising again, and now we're not alone in the hallway anymore. People are moving from one class to another for fourth period or heading to the cafeteria for their lunch.

"Don't you get it? Like, it doesn't matter if I'm the

reason you were mad. Did you mean it? Do you really not care?"

I don't answer. Instead, I stand, staring off down the long corridor.

"Answer me," Stacy persists. "Because seriously? If you love her, that was a super shitty thing to do."

This gets my attention. "Oh yeah? What about you? Aren't you supposed to be her friend?" Sarcasm drips off my tongue.

Stacy shrugs. "Eh, not really. I just basically sit at her lunch table, listening to her and Jenna hold court like they own the place. But whatever." She tosses her long hair over her shoulder and bumps me in the hip. "So, you better figure it out. "

An understatement if ever there was one.

28

Molly

"Could you please not talk to me again? It's for a school project." – Maddie to Brian Bossner after their first and only date

Normally, I am not one to dwell.

I don't pout.

I don't wallow in self-pity.

But there most certainly have been a few occasions when I *have* made exceptions:

The time Erica Pederson cheated off my math test in fifth grade and *I* got in trouble for it. To this day I still can't walk by her in the hall without curling my lip.

1. The time my nanna made me a pig costume for Halloween and my parents forced me to wear it. I was TWELVE.
2. The time Jenna drew a mustache on my face with Sharpie during a sleepover and it wouldn't come off no matter how hard I scrubbed. We had fam-

ily pictures the next day, and I was grounded for a week.

3. Just for dramatic effect, I'm going to repeat the fact that my parents made me wear a pig costume out in public when I was twelve, which we all know is a pivotal point in a young girl's life. I could *easily* have been traumatized by this.

The first thing I want to do, oddly enough, is call my brother. The girly, prideful part of me seriously wants Matthew to come home and kick Weston's ass, maybe rough him up a bit.

Or at least threaten to.

I think that might make me feel better. Right? Ugh, who am I kidding? It would make me feel awful because I don't hate the guy.

I love him.

All the way home, Jenna sits in the passenger seat of the Jeep, and she hasn't said much, which we all know is *so* not like her, but I can definitely hear her muttering under her breath about *all men are creeps,* and how she *should have seen this coming from a guy so hot he could melt ice cream with his hotness.*

Yeah, riveting stuff.

I adjust my seat and shift gears, tuning her out and listening to the sound of my engine and the wind as we cruise down Maple Street, through town, then out onto the country road that leads to my house.

Finally, unable to stand it—because I know Jenna is just *dying* to unleash on me— I say, "So, spill. Tell me what you're really thinking." I take a sidelong look at her, and she's twirling her blonde hair between her neon pink fingertips. The shiny silver thumb ring she's wearing catches the sun, and at first she shakes her head like she's got nothing to say.

But I know better, so I wait.

"I just don't understand it." Jenna turns her body so she's shifted in her seat, facing me. "Why is he doing this? I thought you had this all locked up. Instead, he's being a douche, just like a typical guy."

I tap on the steering wheel and nod. "Well...I guess it just wasn't enough." My words come out just barely above a whisper, sort of raspy.

"Okay, *whatever*, Molly. He can't be one way when you're alone then act like a total dick when he's in public. F *that* shit." The wind whips around us, and Jenna watches me for a few seconds before adding. "So...what are you going to do if he calls?"

I laugh almost bitterly. "He won't call. He's never called."

"Okay, what are you going to do if he *texts*."

Good question. "I have no idea."

"Well you better figure it out, because if I know guys—and I *do* know guys—he is totally going to come crawling back, Molly, and when he does, I want you to be prepared." She flops back in the passenger seat with a loud sigh. "Ugh. This sucks. You didn't even get *laid*."

A short burst of nervous laughter comes out of my mouth in response to her outrageous comment. "Like that was my whole objective. You are *such* a pig!"

Uh, yeah, like the sex thing didn't totally cross my mind.

"I'm serious, Molly, you totally got robbed."

"I wasn't...*with him* so I could get a piece of him, Jenna. I was with him because I genuinely *like* him, and I thought he liked me." I say this so quietly I'm not sure she hears me.

She reaches over to pat the hand that's resting on the gearshift, and I know she understands.

***

The rest of the afternoon drags on. I'm sitting at the counter in the kitchen with my algebra book when my mom bustles in, a brown paper bag of groceries under each of her arms. She gives me a sideways glance, sets the bags down, and turns around with a "Hey."

"Hey back," I say with a forced smile. Mom looks at me for a minute, studying me closely as only a mom will do. I can tell she's trying to figure me out. Am I crabby? Am I sad? Am I just busy with homework?

"Hmm...." she mutters, slightly narrowing her eyes and tilting her head. I swear, if she were an animal, she'd be a predator with the way she's eyeballing me. Finally, she slaps her hands on the counter in front of me. "Okay, what's wrong? Tell your mother. And don't bother saying nothing, because we both know it's a lie."

What is she, a mind reader? Sheesh.

I bite my lip and debate, avoiding eye contact.

"It's that McGrath boy, isn't it?" My mom leans in close. "What did he do?"

My head snaps up. "Nothing!" I practically shout, a little too enthusiastically to be believable. Great. If there's one thing that;s irresistible to a parent, it's denial, so I dial it down a notch. "Technically he didn't do anything."

"So, it's more a case of what he *didn't* do?" Now she's leaning across the counter on her elbows, the groceries behind her already forgotten.

Gee, I hope nothing in those bags is frozen.

Again, I debate about how much to tell my mom, knowing that she's going to tell my dad, and then he'll probably say something to Matthew, because honestly, those two are the *worst* when it comes to gossip, and what girl needs her whole family knowing the details of her love life going up in flames? I hesitate. "Um…"

My mom waits patiently, not saying a word, which is the *worst,* because now I know she's committed to finding out what's going on.

Silent but deadly.

In an attempt to ignore her and avoid any discussion, I click the button on the side of my phone to check for messages, even though I know there isn't one; the indicator light isn't flashing. Heaving out the longest, loudest sigh *ever*, I set it back down on the counter and push it back and forth on the granite while my mom stares me down.

"All right. It's fine if you don't want to talk about it," she finally relents, turning slowly toward the twin paper bags and taking out the first few items. Are her shoulders slumped, or is that just my imagination?

Ugh, I want to scream! Why does she do this?

Now I feel terrible, guilty even.

I sigh again and blow a few stray hairs out of my eyes. "Fine, I'll tell you, but you *cannot* say anything to Dad." My mom flies around and her elbows are immediately back on the counter as she enthusiastically nods and promises her lips are sealed. *I'll believe that one when I see it.*

Finally taking a deep breath, I let it all out, starting from the very beginning.

Weston

Arriving home after a shitty afternoon practice, I bust through the laundry room door and let my hockey gear fall to the ground with a clamorous thud, and it unceremoniously hits the wall. I kick my athletic flip-flops off and throw my hoodie onto a wall hook.

It misses and lands in a heap on the floor.

Wincing when I accidentally smash my shoulder on the doorjamb, I'm rubbing it as I walk into the kitchen, surprised to see my dad standing at the refrigerator. He looks up from digging. "What the hell's with all the ruckus? If you put a dent in the drywall from banging all your shit around, Mom's going to be pissed."

"What are you doing home?" I ask, ignoring his statement. I swing open a cupboard door to grab a glass, filling it with the orange juice my dad has set out on the counter.

"Mom has a dentist appointment, so I grabbed Kendall from school." He looks me over before continuing. "How was practice?"

"Fine. Same shit, different day." Downing the OJ, I'm irritated and he can tell.

"Well that's the winning attitude your mom and I like to see." He rips open a yogurt and throws the top in the trash. "What crawled up your ass?"

Instead of answering, I refill my glass and take another

swig.

"Are you going to tell me what happened at practice, or do we have to stand here all day bullshitting each other?"

"Jeez, does everyone have to ride my nuts?" My dad just stares at me undeterred. He isn't going to let this go. I slouch against the counter, letting my body sag from exhaustion. "It was just a scrimmage, but you know, it was with Whitnall, and they can be real bastards, so we spent the whole damn game fending off high sticks and, as usual, Danberry picked a few fights after someone checked him into the rails."

Again, Dad stares at me. "So I'm gonna ask you again: what is your real problem? And don't tell me it was practice. Is it more shit with that Wakefield girl? Because you know better than to go moping around this house like a goddamn pussy because you let some girl get into your head…"

I slam down my glass, thankful it doesn't break, and storm out of the kitchen.

"Don't you walk away from me, god dammit. Get your ass back here now so we can talk about this," my dad bellows, his deep baritone voice vibrating through the first floor of the house. From upstairs I can hear a bedroom door open, and Kendall's head appears from around the banister railing.

"Oooh, oooh, you are in troublllle…" she sings in a loud whisper. I roll my eyes, pivoting to stalk back into the kitchen for a confrontation.

The temptation to punch a wall is overwhelming, but instead I lean lazily against the counter, crossing my arms and projecting an *I don't give a shit what you're about to say* attitude.

My dad points an index finger at me. "Look, I don't give a shit if you're going to date or not"—I snort when he says this—"but once you let it affect your schoolwork or your game, you're done."

Now I'm rolling my eyes.

"Don't fucking stand there and roll your eyes at me, and don't tell me this girl hasn't gotten into your head. Since when do you come home throwing shit around the house and being disrespectful? Huh?"

"Big deal if I tossed my shit down. I had a shitty day, what do you care?"

My dad studies me for a while without responding, and it finally makes me so uncomfortable, I cross and uncross my arms a few times while I'm standing there in defense mode.

My dad continues, "You're going to stand there and ask why I care? Who do you think paid for all those hockey lessons and ran you to practice? Do you think that was a goddamn cake walk?" He pauses. "Now, without getting all pissed off, tell me what's really going on with you." He leans back against the fridge and crosses his arms so he's mirroring me, and I can't help but feel like I'm looking into my own future. I actually find myself wondering if someday I'll be lecturing my own kid about the same stupid crap.

Running my palm down the front of my face, I have no actual idea where to start, so I say, "This actually has nothing to do with…" Oh Christ, why is it so hard to say her name? "Molly. It mostly has to do with, I don't know… other people giving me shit about her. Hockey. School."

Dad is nodding his head slowly and not saying anything, so I take this as a good sign and continue. "So, I always have all these girls after me, right, which has always driven me crazy, nothing new there, but now that I've gone out with someone and we really hit it off…and all these other girls haven't gone away…and my friends are such assholes. It's just…" I let out a loud, frustrated "Gruuuhhh!" that actually comes out sounding like a grunt and a scream.

"Wes, are you and Molly having sex?"

"What! No. Why would you ask that? When she was here did she *look* like the type of girl who would just spread 'em for anyone? Jeez."

"Son, I hate to break it to you, but no girl looks like the type when they're soaking wet, unless of course they're wearing a swim suit."

"We are *not* having sex."

"Well then, maybe *that's* your damn problem." My dad grins while he rubs the stubble on his chin. He pushes himself off the fridge and checks his watch. "Look, date Molly or don't date her, but once you start getting off track…" He runs his hand across his throat in a *you're cut off* motion. "And for God's sake, don't let anyone else influence you, unless it's your Mom or me." He laughs at his own joke. "Oh, and Weston? Stop being such a little prick around here. You're driving us nuts." He grabs his keys off the counter and walks into the living room to bellow up the stairs. "Kendall, let's get rolling. You have soccer in twenty."

And that, folks, is about as warm and fuzzy as it gets with Brian McGrath. He and Kendall leave, and I'm still standing in the kitchen in the same spot where he left me. I run a hand over my face just as my stomach growls.

Resigned, I sigh loudly, dig my cell out of the back pocket of my cargo shorts, and text the only person I can think of who will be around.

29

Molly

"What you put up with, you end up with." – Mrs. Wakefield

I am starving.

And pathetically, I am at the one place where I shouldn't be. Not only *that*, but I'm alone. Completely and utterly alone. I couldn't even convince Jenna to take pity on me enough to come along. That traitor.

She tossed me over for Alex, who has a band concert tonight.

Yeah, that's right, you heard me correctly.

A *band* concert.

What's even worse: Alex doesn't even play a manly instrument. Nope. He plays the clarinet, and hey, no offense to any of you clarinet players, but come on, he's a guy. Although now that I think about it, the guy does wear skinny jeans…

Whatever, Jenna hates noodles anyway.

I pull the romance book out of my bag—it's been weeks since I've had time to read anything—and slap it on the table, followed by my iPod and cell phone. Tucked away in a corner booth, I don't know how I ended up at Kyoto, but my Jeep—of its own accord, mind you—seemed to be on autopilot, because before I even knew what was happening, I was driving myself here. Call me crazy. Call me a glutton for punishment. *I just couldn't seem to help myself.*

So here I sit, admittedly a little glum. Cracking open my book, which shall remain nameless—the title is simply too embarrassing to reveal—I lean back and settle in, forking my plate idly to let the steam out of my heaping pile of veggies and noodles. The steam rises to drift up to the hanging lamp above, and I can't resist musing that if Weston were here, he wouldn't hesitate to shove a forkful into his impatient mouth.

I smile ruefully as my phone pings and the new text, not surprisingly, is from Jenna.

Her: *Help. Seriously. I want to poke my eyes out.*

Me: *Awww, what a good gf u are*

Jenna: *This isn't funny. Omg did u know rachel davenport plays the tuba? Shoot me now.*

No, actually I didn't know Rachel Davenport played the tuba. Yeah, it is a rather odd choice for someone so short, but what do I care?

Me: *U really should be paying more attention. Tsk tsk*

Jenna: *I hate you.*

Chuckling, I get back to my book and give my noodles a little poke every now and again, my stomach growling in protest. It wants to eat. Huffing a sigh at myself for my own impatience, I lean forward and pick up my fork. As I'm slowly twirling the long whole-wheat noodles around the tines, I glance up briefly toward the door and swear my eyes are playing a horrible, hideous trick on me. Since God has never answered my previous prayers about opening up the earth and letting it swallow me whole, I don't even bother chanting the request in my head.

I look up at the door again and rub my eyes with my free hand.

Nope, this is not a dream.

It's a nightmare.

Weston and his buddies are most *definitely* standing in the entry of the restaurant's dining room, scanning for a free table. At the front of the group, Derek Hanson elbows that guy, Adam Something-or-other, and they both stare in my direction. I slink lower in my seat, grasping and fumbling for my ear buds and shoving them into my ears, hitting the power button on my iPod in a futile attempt to drown out any conversation of theirs I might pick up on.

Then, in an act of even further desperation, I hold my book in front of my face, sleazy romantic cover be damned. Beggars can't be choosers, after all, and I can't hold my napkin in front of my face.

Oh my God, I can't imagine how stupid I look. I can't even think about it without getting ill.

Shit, shit, double SHIT.

Weston

Obviously I can see Molly in the corner of the restaurant,

and from the looks of it, she is one camper who is not happy to see me. I study her for a few brief seconds while my friends make snide comments beside me, and she kind of actually reminds me of this one time I took Kendall to the zoo and they let us hold a baby chinchilla. First the tiny little critter avoided all eye contact from the corner of its cage, then once I picked it up, it pretended to be dead.

"Guys, check it out. Stalker alert, one o'clock," Derek jokes loudly, smacking Adam in the arm and pointing toward Molly's table. A hollow pit forms in my stomach, because the jackass was so loud there is no doubt she heard him.

"What, like there are no other places to eat around here?" Erik Travers chimes in, and I immediately lose any respect I had for him, labeling him a follower and adding him to my shit list, mentally noting to take him out at tomorrow's practice.

"Dude, you know a chick's desperate when she—"

"Would you assholes mind *shutting* the fuck up?" Rick comes up behind me, growling at our small party of teammates. "Keep it up, pansies, and I'll have you skating suicides on a day we don't have practice." Rick claps his large hand on my shoulder. "You dickheads go sit down. I wanna talk to McGrath real quick."

I move to go sit, but he stops me with a hand on my chest. "Why don't you just go over there, for crap's sake? You look like someone kicked your puppy."

"Because I keep fucking up by saying all the wrong shit. She hates me." If I didn't know any better, I would say my shoulders were sagging a little from both exhaustion *and* defeat.

"Jesus *Christ,* do you sound like a girl," Rick says, his lip curling in disgust.

"What do you even care? I thought you were pissed at me," I mumble, glancing over my shoulder to watch Molly hiding behind her book.

"Well damn, it's better than watching you mope. I might be a prick, and I might not really give a shit about your feelings, but I want to win games, and dude, for the past few days you've royally sucked."

"Gee, Rick, tell me how you really feel."

"Since you asked, I guess I *could* be apologizing for my asshole behavior with Molly. I guess I didn't realize you were seriously interested. Plus, let's be honest, I kind of have a huge ego." Rick shrugs and claps me on the back.

"Please stop before you end up hugging me and I have to punch you in the nuts."

Molly

"The right guy will move mountains to be with you; he won't hide behind them." – Mandy Hale

My once healthy appetite has completely deserted me as I hover in the safety of this booth, too anxious to even look up. My mind takes a turn, and I can't help but wonder how long I'm going to be stuck here, rendered helpless by the group of boys across the room. Even though I have a book in front of my face, I can totally sense that they're watching me. "50 Ways to Say Goodbye" by Train pumps through my iPod, drowning out any conversation, and for that I am thankful, but honestly, this is way worse than one of those dreams where you're naked in front of a crowd.

"Mind if I keep you company?"

Please God, let the earth open up and swallow me whole, I pray, *like, as in* right *freaking now.*

Seriously.

I look up to see Weston standing there in his masculine glory, staring down at me with expectation in his eyes, one hand holding his dinner and one hand stuffed in the pocket of his black Adidas athletic pants. His hair is wet, presumably from the shower he took after practice.

A lump forms in my throat, and I have to clear it and swallow hard to keep from blurting out all the things I want to say. Sensing my hesitation, Weston looks over his shoulder at the guys, and Rick Stevens shoos him with his hand as if to say, *Go on, bro*. Knotting my brow in confusion, I set my book down and look back up at Weston.

"Please, Molly," he says. Well, I can't really hear him because of the music in my ears, but I can read it on his lips. Because I'm stubborn, I say nothing. To be fair, I don't feel like there is anything *to* say. I mean, he said it all in the hallway when he made it clear that I meant nothing to him…right? I bite my lower lip and look down at the table.

"What are you listening to?" he prompts, pointing to my ear buds.

I shake my head.

Nope.

Not giving in.

Okay, maybe I'll just turn the volume way down, in case he says something meaningful. Sensing a weakness in my fortitude, Weston artfully slides into the booth with a grace that still surprises me for a guy his size. Then, just like he always does, he sets his plate down, unrolls his utensils from the paper napkin, and places his fork on the left side of the plate, knife on the right.

Smiling, he takes a bite of his noodles, but not before scalding himself in the process. A sick part of me is glad he just scalded his mouth, and as he frantically grabs his water glass, I feel a smile threatening to break free. To hide it, I reach for my own glass and take a drink.

He swallows, clears his throat, then says, "We really have to stop meeting like this." He thrusts his hand out across the table for me to shake it, and I stare at him like he's grown a second head. "Okay, let me rephrase that. Hi, I'm Wes, and for the past few weeks I've treated someone I really care about like shit, so I'm here to apologize."

"Yet again."

"Huh?"

"Apologize *yet again*. Correct me if I'm wrong, but this is what…the third time?" I tick off three fingers and thrust my hand at him. "You know the rule, Weston: three strikes, you're *out*." I push my fork around my plate to find some veggies. As I take a quick bite of my cold dinner, I cringe. Newsflash: noodles taste hideous when they're cold.

"Wait, was that a baseball reference?"

I roll my eyes at him. "Don't be an ass. You *know* what I meant."

Weston

Yeah. I know what she means, but *clearly* I am trying to divert her attention. She's fixated on being pissed at me, and it sucks. "Sorry. I'm not trying to be an ass on purpose. Sometimes it just happens."

"Yeah, well, I guess that's why we aren't friends anymore."

Ouch, that hurt.

Molly cocks an eyebrow at stares at me, lobbing a challenge across the table at full force. I grab it and volley back, "I wouldn't be sitting here groveling if I didn't want to be *friends*." I stress the word friends, hoping my tone is suggestive.

"I wouldn't exactly call what you're doing *groveling*. If that's what this is, it's pretty pathetic." She takes another bite of noodles and chews slowly.

I really don't think Molly has a clue how hard it was for me to come over here—especially with a table of my friends nearby, friends who have turned into spectators and who, with a quick glance, I can see are watching us intently. So even though I'm sitting here making wise-cracks, my stomach is in knots and my palms are sweaty.

I wipe them on my jeans and take a deep breath. "You're the wind that swept me off my feet. Say we made it through the storm. Here comes the sun, here comes the rain."

For a few moments, Molly just sits and stares at me with a really confused look on her face. Then, as if a light goes off inside her head, she launches her body to the corner of the booth and begins laughing her ass off, gasping for breath. "Oh my God," she eventually pants. "You did *not* just quote Bridgit Mendler!"

My face gets bright red, and because I'm embarrassed, it feels like she is practically shouting. "Would you please keep your voice down? *People* are listening." And by people, I mean my dickhead friends who would never in a million *years* let me forget something like quoting a cheesy pop star to earn forgiveness from a girl.

"Say more, say more. *Please*," Molly begs.

"Oh great, I'm really glad you think it's so freaking hilarious. Well guess what, smartass, it's *not*. It's how I *feel*." I cross my arms indignantly as she watches me, studying my face with a scrunched-up mouth. Then, just when I think she's going to drop the subject—or at least take pity on me—Molly busts out in hysterics a second time. In fact, she's laughing so hard I'm pretty sure there are actual tears coming out of her eyes. For about five more minutes, I sit here seething and silently wishing I had kept my mouth shut.

I could seriously curse the fact that I've taken dating advice from Kendall, of all people. In fact, what was it she said to me as I was leaving the house this afternoon? *"Girls like when you say mushy stuff to them, Wes, like movie quotes and junk. They think it's romantic. Here, take this CD and listen to it. It has some super good material."*

That 'super good material' happened to be her new Bridgit Mendler CD, and, being the good brother that I am, I considered it my duty to at *least* give it a listen. Like I said, I'm an idiot for taking advice from an eleven-year-old—especially from one with a peculiar delight in making me look like the world's biggest ass in public.

Across from me, Molly is wiping her eyes and grinning at me, which I take as a good sign. At least she's not trying to stab me with her butter knife or crafting a voodoo doll of me in her free time.

"In my defense, that was all Kendall's idea," I finally say, picking up the paper napkin on my tray and ripping off the end pieces.

"You went to Kendall for help?" Molly tilts her head and studies me. Her eyes go a little soft around the edges as she says, "Aw, that's kind of sweet...in a totally weird sort of way. I mean, come on, Weston, she's eleven. Of *course* she's going have you listening to some star from *Good Luck, Charlie*. Heck, you're lucky she didn't have you listening to One Direction. Now *that* would have been an embarrassing train wreck."

"Thanks a lot. Thank you, as if I wasn't aware of that."

"Well, then why would you—"

Interrupting her I say, "Listen, Molly. If I'm taking advice from my little sister, someone who really likes you and wants us to be...um, *together*...and she tells me to quote lyrics from a pop singer, well, that's what I'm going to do, because I'm that serious. I want to try again, and I want this to work."

Molly

I study Weston for a few seconds, my heart beating out of my chest. Okay. He's definitely got my attention with all this try-again-and-make-this-work talk. "So what other advice did Kendall give you? You know, since you brought it up and all..."

Weston takes a minute to think, and a slow grin almost lights up his face, but then he glances over his shoulder across the restaurant to where his friends sit watching us with intense interest. A disdainful scowl mars his handsome face as he shoots a look in their direction for good measure before focusing his attention back on me. For the record, his friends *clearly* don't give a crap, because they're at their table laughing like a pack of hyenas, each guy laughing louder than the next.

He clears his throat and grins again in the cutest, almost bashful way. "She overheard me talking to my dad the other day and cornered me in the hallway last night when she was supposed to be in bed." Weston grins at the memory. "She actually had it all written out on a sheet of paper. So besides the advice about singing you a song—aren't you glad I spared you having to listen to me sing?—she also suggested the following: writing you a love poem, throwing rocks at your bedroom window in the middle of the night, and let's see, what else…decorating your locker with rose petals."

I chuckle at that one. "Wow, she has quite the imagination."

"I'm not done yet," he says, and he ticks off the suggestions on his fingers. "Declaring my love during the pep rally next week, which actually isn't a bad idea…"

Laughing, I add, "Don't you dare!"

"What's the next best thing, Molly?" Weston asks, getting serious. "What's it going to take for you to forget the shitty things I said?"

"It's not like I want this to be a big, dramatic thing, Wes. I just think you aren't ready to date anyone, and I… think *I* might be. Finally, you know? It's been four years of high school of me just watching from the outside, going on a few shitty dates and to dances with guys as just friends, and I'm done doing that." I play with my straw. "In a few months we're going to be leaving for college. Imagine all those parties. All those single guys…" I sigh dramatically, let my voice trail off, and rest my chin in my elbow.

Am I being manipulative? Probably, but who's here to stop me? Besides, when I report all of this back to Jenna, the details better be juicy or I'm in deep shit. I better make this good.

"Wait—what parties? What single guys?" he asks, frowning. I waggle my eyebrows at him, which makes him turn a deep shade of pink. "That's not fucking funny, Molly."

"Let's get real for a minute, Weston. Not once did we discuss being exclusive, and not *once* did I call you my boyfriend or act like you suddenly were. So, I don't get why you went into panic mode each time someone brought it up. Newsflash, buddy! It was kind of insulting."

He has the decency to look embarrassed and stutters, "I'm... I'm..."

I believe the word he's looking for here is *sorry*.

I let him squirm.

Tilting my head, I wait while he fumbles with his apology. "Molly, I'm an idiot. What do you want me to say? I'm eighteen and I've never had a girlfriend. I've been on one date, except that one with you. I've never bought anyone flowers, I've never had sex with anyone I care about, and I've never brought anyone home to meet my parents. I have no goddamn clue what I'm doing, okay?" He stares at me. When I don't answer, he says again, "Okay?"

Not convinced, I purse my lips. "Yeah, but still...."

"There was one other thing Kendall mentioned doing that I think might work to get back into your good graces: a grand gesture." He leans back and puts his arms behind his head, thinking.

"Grand *gesture*? What did she mean by that?"

"You're asking *me*? Shit, I had to Google it." Suddenly, without warning, he stands up at the table, his whole body jostling the surface and causing everything on it to shake and clatter. Clearing his throat, Weston loudly says, "Excuse me, excuse me, can I have your attention?"

Besides his table of teammates, about five other people turn to stare at us.

Holy shit, he is not about to—

"Attention, please," he repeats. While I'm horrified by what's about to happen, a sick part of me kind of wants to hear what he's about to say. He continues, "My name is Weston, and I've been a complete idiot."

His friends begin shouting in agreement, and loud insults are being hurled at Weston as he stands. "Boo! Sit down, douchebag!" "McGrath is a pansy ass!" My personal favorite, yelled across the room by Rick, is "Hey, McGrath, your mommy called and wants her tampon back!"

I leap up and grab his arm to stop him. His strong, muscular, tanned arm… "Oh my god, please sit down. I'm *begging* you." I hiss at him in a sharp whisper. He looks down at my hand on his arm and gives his head a quick shake.

"I have to do this, Molly. For you."

Oh, brother. Someone's obviously been knocked over the head with the dip stick.

Gag me.

There is, of course, nothing I can do but watch.

Weston

"According to your own calculations, this is strike three. I say, if she's willing to give you yet another chance, she's a real keeper. Now go be a man and prove to her why she should keep you around…you dipshit." – Brian McGrath

Now everyone in the entire place is staring. Granted, there aren't all that many people here to begin with, thank God, but still. From the corner of my eye, I can see Rick punch someone in the arm, and I hear a loud, staged shush from somewhere in the room. Undaunted, I reach into my pocket and pull out a crinkled sheet of paper, carefully opening it and working out the creases by running it over my knee a few times. If you're thinking to yourself, *Wow, this dude is prepared. I bet he was a Boy Scout*, you'd be wrong. Good guess though.

Clearing my throat in a now silent restaurant dining room, I begin reading the letter Kendall has prepared. "Dear Molly, I am writing this so you will give my brother another chance, even though he keeps saying some really dumb stuff. Please don't blame him. He gets hit in the face a lot with hockey sticks." I look down at Molly then over at my friends, who are cackling and falling over each other with laughter. Lee Bricker is rolling around on the floor as I continue. "Not only that, I'm pretty sure most of his teeth are fake. Wait. What?"

Shit, maybe I should have read this before I started reading it. I glance at Molly and grumble, "That's totally not true." Damn little sisters.

I continue.

"But no matter what he said or did to make you mad, you should know that he really likes you. And even though one time he ate an entire batch of cookies my mom made for my birthday party at school—gee, thanks, Kendall— he's the best brother a girl could have. And he wants you to be his girlfriend, even if he won't say it, because he's a boy, and we all know that boys are, well, dumb."

Everyone is laughing—some hysterically—and clapping as I finish the letter and begin folding it back up into a neat little square. Before I can stick it back in my pocket, Molly reaches for it.

"Please, can I have that?" Her eyes are smiling, even if her mouth is in a serious straight line.

"What are you planning on doing? Burning it in a bonfire pit?"

She smirks. "Maybe, maybe not."

I hold it out but snatch it back before she can take hold of it. "I'll only give this to you if you promise you're going to put it under your pillow."

Inwardly I groan at how stupid it sounds when I'm trying to be slick, and Molly rolls her eyes heavenward. "Why? Is the tooth fairy gonna come?"

"More like the boyfriend fairy," I snicker slyly.

From across the room, my friends are shouting, "Dude, we can hear you!" and "You sound like a fucking idiot!" Not to be outdone, Gavin Woznuski is chanting "Douche!" over and over, banging on the table with his fists.

"Please ignore them," I say grimly as my face gets warm from the blush creeping up my neck.

"Hmmm, I don't know. They are pretty hard to ignore," Molly muses, tapping her chin in thought.

Molly

Before I'm even close to finishing my next thought, Weston grabs my hand in front of everyone, half-dragging me across the restaurant until we are in the parking lot, leaning against my car.

The street lights above us flicker as they struggle to turn on, and Weston hovers over me. He taps on the back window of my Jeep. "That back seat is looking mighty good to me right now…" His voice trails off suggestively.

I glance over his shoulder and take in our audience. His friends have their faces practically pressed against the glass of Kyoto. Rick is blowing on the glass, puffing his cheeks up and completely disgusting me in the process.

I roll my eyes at his suggestion and laugh. "Even without an audience, you sound awfully confident for someone who was groveling not ten minutes ago." Still, the idea of kissing him in the car has merit, and old habits die hard as I begin playing with the collar of his worn T-shirt. Pulling at a loose thread and letting the tip of my finger stroke the smooth skin above his collar, Weston groans and buries his face in my hair.

He inhales deeply and lets out a breath. "I missed you."

"Good."

He pulls back sharply to look at me. "What the hell!"

"Well, I want you to remember that feeling next time you run your mouth off to other people. Seriously, Jenna was about to come castrate you."

Weston leans forward and kisses my collarbone, muttering, "Castration isn't very nice."

"No, but at least she's got my back."

"I'd like to get you *on* your back…"

"Hey! I haven't said I'm giving you another chance." I pull a straight face and tip my chin up defiantly.

"Babe, please. I promise I won't run away like a chicken shit again. I just need you to know that I'm an asshole, and that's probably not going go to change…I mean, look at my dad. Hello."

I don't say anything, but I do make a *hmmph* sound in my throat.

"Molly, can you just love me for the asshole I am?"

"Well…when you put it that way, how could I possibly resist?"

Epilogue

Weston

"Let me know what happens at the end. Call me or some shit." – Rick Stevens

Here we are, one year later, although it seems like just yesterday we were standing in that parking lot, my heart beating out of my chest as I waited anxiously to hear if Molly was going to give me another chance.

I check my watch one more time, noting that if we don't head out now, we aren't going to make it on time. "Molly, babe, let's go!" I call up the stairs. "If you're not down in five seconds, I'm coming up."

"Babe, I'm coming!" she shouts back. "Two more seconds." I can hear low mumbled curses and her hopping around frantically on one foot, probably trying to pull boots on or something.

A voice interrupts me from behind. "Oh my god, dude, every time I hear you two 'babe-ing' each other, it makes me want to blow chunks," Matthew Wakefield says, walking into the foyer and shoving a fistful of almonds into his mouth.

"Hey, give me a couple of those," I demand.

He slaps my hand away, quite viciously I might add, and sticks the bag of almonds in the pocket of his hoodie. "Get your own damn delicious treats. Jeez, bro, isn't it enough that I have to put up with your crap at school? Now you're stealing shit from me in my own home? Back off."

Yeah. You heard that correctly.

You're looking at a freshman starter for the Wisconsin Badgers Hockey team, and I guess you could say the bane of Matthew Wakefield's existence. Actually, Molly and I *both* go to Madison now and are only home this weekend for the homecoming hockey game—which, of course, we're running late for.

Just as I'm saying, "Can you tell your sister to please get her sweet ass down here?" Molly comes racing down the hallway and down the stairs.

Out of breath, she leans into me and greets me by planting her soft lips on mine. "Mmm, thanks for waiting." My arms immediately go to her butt and I pull her in.

"Don't I get a hello?" Matthew complains and nudges his sister in the arm like a Neanderthal. "Hey, get your hands off her ass."

"Shhh, go away, I'm saying hello to my boyfriend."

"Seriously, knock it off or I'll tell Dad you were fornicating in the foyer."

Molly reaches around me and swats at her brother. "Go away, Matty."

It never ends with these two.

"Fine, but just so you know, I'll be listening." Matthew points to his ears, giving me a piercing look before stalking off toward the living room with his bag of almonds.

"Finally, I thought he'd *never* leave," I whisper.

"Do we *really* have to see the game?" Molly pouts, pushing my sweatshirt up and sticking her warm hands under my many layers. "We could stay home and do other... *stuff.*"

Not gonna lie: in the year we've been dating, I've become one horny bastard. Having a steady girlfriend is great, because I get to have sex with my best friend—like, all the time. For a second there I almost give in to her hands roaming my bare chest. One thing is for sure: if she's trying to manipulate the situation so we'll stay home by getting me turned on, it's *almost* working.

"I can solve this problem by dragging you upstairs for a quickie. You do know that, right?"

Hmm, guess she hadn't thought of that. "Ugh, fine. Forget it, let's go."

I laugh at her, pouting. "This is why I love you."

She leans up and kisses me when I pull the front door open. "Ah, baby, I love you too."

"I can hear you. Get the hell out of here already! I'm totally disgusted!" Matthew shouts from the living room.

Holding hands, we walk out the door.

Preview the next book in the Kiss and Make Up Series:

HE KISSED me FIRST

SARA NEY

Prologue

Cecelia

"Do you ever wish you could just *un*-meet someone?" – me, wishfully thinking

Have you ever had a story to tell but just couldn't figure out a good way to start it? That seems to be my life these days: a veritable daily struggle-fest (as my little sister Veronica would say). Absolutely nothing has gone right for me today.

Nothing.

Allow me to tell you about the craptastic morning I first met Matthew Wakefield.

First, I didn't climb out of bed with grace. No. I stumbled. Of course, I still had my eye mask on (that's right haters, I wear an eye mask; it's not a crime, so get over it). Instead of peeling it off like a normal person, I blindly reached for the table next to my bed so I could balance myself before standing up, missed by a mile—naturally—

smashed into that, and managed to knock over the lamp on my desk (the light bulb shattered; thanks for caring) which, incidentally, is halfway across the room.

Really quickly, can I note that at *no* point during all this loud crashing and banging around did anyone come to check on me (thanks Mom and Dad).

So yeah.

After that little introduction to my morning, let's fast forward a bit, to when I backed my car into my parents' recycling bins, had no change for a toll at the state line of Wisconsin and Illinois, and to top it all off, didn't pass a single McDonald's.

So it shouldn't surprise me that:

1. I am a hot mess. Hair falling out of my top knot, mascara smudges under both my eyes, and—bonus!—I just caught a faint whiff of myself, and all I have to say is…grody. I'm mostly sweaty and gross from lugging my damn bags, and it really would be tougher to get any grosser than this—*unless* you count the fact that there's almost a 100% certainty that my underwear are on inside out. #ratchet

2. I hashtagged myself. Deal with it.

3. I. Am. Starving, and my stomach will not let me forget it—it's all knotted up and growling, and my legs have also decided to start shaking from my plummeting blood sugar level. Wonderful. I'm pretty darn sure if you saw me on the street you'd think I was on *crack*.

4. My mom has been text bombing me since I left. Either she thinks I've been murdered, *or* she must have found the lamp…and the smashed light

bulb. *Oops.* Oh well, the lamp was ugly anyway.

Lugging my tote down the long corridor in my apartment building, I fumble for the keys I've foolishly placed in my back pocket, and in the process drop my phone, sunglasses, purse, and several books I'd been holding on to by a thread.

Great.

Peachy.

Awesome.

The bag slung over my shoulder is so heavy it's weighing me down, thus creating no real way to bend down and pick up all my crap without also dropping the bag and/or injuring myself in the process.

This bag is *that* heavy.

It is actually dragging down the neckline of my plain white t-shirt, which I'm sure looks just *fab*ulous.

Cripes, why did I pack so much for the long weekend? It looks like I've packed enough to move back home, when really it's just a few pair of shoes, some jeans, shirts, underwear, a few bras, more books, makeup, curling iron, um… blow-dryer, robe, a few DVDs…oh, and a water bottle and workout clothes. I think I tossed my laptop in there too. Also, er, hairspray, a brush, and a comb, but those hardly take up any space.

Plus extra tote and slippers.

Eye mask…

All right, all right! You get the picture.

I try digging in my back pocket again and wonder what possessed me to wear such tight pants this morning (oh that's right…*they look awesome on me)* and end up palming the small wad of twenty dollar bills my mom surreptitiously stuffed into my pocket when I left this morning. Originally, she tried to get my *dad* to give me the extra cash, but as usual, he only pulled out one ten-dollar bill.

"Roger, that's not even enough for some snacks at a gas station!" my mom shouted at my dad from across the driveway.

To which my dad (aka Roger) replied, "She's almost twenty-three years old Margot; I would think at this point we wouldn't *need* to be supporting her."

My mom just shot him a dirty look, adding, "At least give her a hug good-bye."

I'll be honest: Roger always needs a reminder. He's not much for public displays of affection. I'm his daughter for crying out loud, and he blushes every time he is forced to hug me—not that I blame him. My grandparents weren't really affectionate either, and obviously the trait has been passed down to my dad.

Poor guy.

I'm the opposite, and my favorite thing to do is grab him, lock him in a bear hug, and squish him until he shoves me off.

It can get awkward sometimes, but a little awkward never hurt anybody.

You can quote me on that.

As I get closer to my apartment door, I breath a loud sigh of relief because hallelujah! I can hear the voice of my roommate inside. Although…it kind of sounds like she's arguing with someone. But hey, at least she's inside, because I'll probably need a hand with my stuff.

Instead of knocking, I bang the door with my hip, using all my might to heave the heavy tote like a wrecking ball so it slams into the door with a *thunk*.

I give a meek little "Help" and wait.

And wait.

Inside I hear a bang, like someone's smashed into an end table or desk, then I hear an "oomph" followed immediately by a groan.

Weird, and totally out of the ordinary.

Slightly panicked, I again bang on the door again with my hip, drop my bag, and fumble frantically for my keys.

Matthew

What the *shit* is that banging?

I look at my little sister Molly and she shrugs, trudging toward the door. I put my arm out to stop her. "Don't you *dare* get that—it's obviously some lunatic."

Molly rolls her eyes at me (the little brat) like she is always doing—and when I say always, I mean she's *constantly* rolling her eyes. I'm surprised they haven't gotten lodged permanently in the back of her head.

"It's either a lunatic or it's my roommate, so get out of my way you Neanderthal. This is *my* apartment."

Using all her strength (and trust me, she might appear scrawny, but she's way stronger than she looks), Molly manages to shove me out of her way, even as I attempt to block her path. In my attempts to stall her, my leg connects with the blue Rubbermaid bin she and her roomie have disguised as a coffee table, and the shit piled on top of it falls to the carpet.

Correction: the *dirty* carpet.

"Don't you dare open that door without finding out who it is first," I warn, sounding like our dad, while bending to scoop up a handful of Cosmo magazines from the floor. Kate Upton stares back at me from an August issue, and I stop reorganizing for a brief moment to admire her ample chest.

Damn she's good-lookin'.

Without hesitating, I start thumbing through the magazine, momentarily distracted by its contents. Shit, if the rest of these pictures are anything like Kate Upton's cover, I just might consider rolling this baby up and stuffing it into my back pocket.

"The door has no peephole, *moron*. Hey, stop touching my stuff! God you are so *annoy*ing," Molly huffs in outrage, boldly slapping the magazine out of my hand. "I still don't know why you're even here."

I shrug, not giving a shit about her bad manners. She truly sounds disgusted with me. "Why the hell are you in a building that has no peepholes? That's not safe. The least your landlord can do given these shoddy doors—which are basically made out of plywood—is put in some damn peepholes."

"Oh my gawd, you are such an idiot. Please say peepholes one more freaking time."

"Whoa, whoa, whoa, one insult at a time please. Can you stop being such a bitch for two seconds?" I ask, bending over a *second* time to rescue Kate Upton. Her boobs have gotten wrinkled from being dropped twice, and I pause to smooth out her pages.

It's the least I can do.

Then, before I can stop her, Molly uses a self-defense move *I* taught her and swiftly elbows me in the gut with a jab so quick I don't even see it coming.

Grunting, I teeter a bit and hold my stomach before I can stand upright. "That was a cheap shot," I croak out as the banging on the door gets louder. It sounds like someone's trying to break through the damn door with battering ram.

"What the *fuck?*" I march toward the door, palming Molly in the forehead to halt her and steeling myself against a possible assault. "Back *down* Molly. Christ. Do you really think Weston would want you charging the door when some mental person is on the other side banging it in? Step aside dammit."

She moves aside, biting her lip.

Well shit, that was easy.

At the simple mention of her pansy ass boyfriend's name, Molly's shoulders sag a little and she crosses her arms. I can tell she's debating about whether or not to give in as she continues chewing on her lower lip with a furrowed brow, deep in concentration.

I make a mental note to use Weston as my war strategy in the future.

Stalking to the door, I unlatch the deadbolt and throw it open, fist clenched at my side, ready to sucker punch someone in the face if necessary.

I open my mouth but don't have the chance to speak because I'm shoved aside by the girl standing in the hallway. With a giant mop of brown hair piled on the top of her head (that could honestly be a dead animal for all I know), smeared eye makeup giving her raccoon eyes, and a death glare, she pushes past me and demands shrilly, "Hey buddy, what the hell is going on in here? I could hear noises out in the hall."

Aw shit. She's kind of scary, actually.

The tall brunette rushes to my sisters' side, grabbing Molly by the shoulders and giving her a little shake. "Molly, are you okay? Is this guy bothering you?" the interloper demands, only turning for a quick second to shoot me another scowl and dump a pile of crap on to the couch—a pile, I can't help but noticing, that includes a bag of trail mix and a bag of Sun Chips.

Which reminds me, I'm *crazy* hungry.

"Yup. I was just trying to get him to leave, but he refuses." Molly, the little traitor, shoots me a triumphant look over her friend's head and winks.

Fucking *winks*.

Wait. *What?* "Hey! Now wait just one damn minute—"

The girl snorts indignantly out of her pert little nose and steps forward to jam her finger into my solid chest, so hard I can feel her nail. "No pal, *you* wait one damn minute. This is *my* apartment and Molly wants *you* gone, so it's time for you to go before I *pepper spray* your ass. Get out into the hallway and keep your hands where I can see them."

What. The. Fu…*ck*.

Out of the corner of my eye, I see my little sister continuing to smirk, her laughing eyes betraying her attempts to get me to leave. She's clearly incredibly entertained and therefore in no hurry to set this chick (who is *obviously* bat-shit crazy) straight.

I'm seriously going to murder Molly. Then when I'm

done, I'm going to dig up her dead, lifeless body and kill her all over again. Ah shit, do I sound bitter?

"Who the hell *are* you, anyway?" I ask.

"Who the hell am *I*? Hey, *I'll* be asking the questions, thank you very much. Hallway please. Seriously, I might be thin, but I have a black belt."

"Black belt?" Crossing my arms, I chuckle snidely. "Somehow, I seriously doubt that, so please don't make me laugh." I walk over to the couch and flop down on it. "What are you, a hundred and thirty pounds soaking wet?" I dismissively palm through the girl's discarded pile of stuff and snatch up the bag of trail mix from where it was sandwiched between a textbook and a curling iron. Without hesitating, I take custody of it and rip the plastic bag open savagely with my teeth—I mean, it was just *lying* there in the pile.

"Sweet, trail mix, my favorite."

"What are you doing, you *jack*ass!" Molly's irrational roommate-slash-bodyguard screeches (loudly I might add), trying to grab the bag out of my hands.

I hold it above my head out of her reach and flash her my pearly whites while looking her up and down. "You really ought to stop throwing yourself at me—it's embarrassing. Sorry, but you're not my type. Maybe if you cleaned yourself up a bit…"

I crunch down on a handful of nuts and pretzels, chewing noisily.

"Get the hell *out* of here!" the roommate fumes, white knuckles clenched at her sides. I can practically *see* the steam rising from her ears.

"Hey now, don't get defensive, I'm just the messenger," I soothe.

"Are you hearing me, asshole? I said get the hell out."

"You should listen to her, Matthew." Molly agrees with a shit-eating grin. She's leaning against the kitchen counter now, poking idly through a candy dish.

Ignoring them both and enjoying this scenario immensely, I spread my legs wide on the couch, tip my head back, and shake more trail mix into my mouth from the bag, which basically means it's mine now.

Fact: possession is nine-tenths of the law.

"Thanks for the snack," I say as I eat the last crumb and emit a satisfied groan. "I'll pay you back."

Or not.

I crumble the empty bag and toss it onto the coffee table, stretch my arms out behind my head, and groan again. "Mmm, that hit the spot. I was starving."

The roommate's mouth falls open, and for a brief moment she's actually silent. Thank god. I take advantage, adding, "Next time can you stock up on the Costco brand of trail mix? I like it much better than this gas station crap you bought."

"Oh my god, you are so rude! So *rude*! What the hell is your problem? *Get out!*" Again from the roommate in a high-pitched shriek.

All this squawking is giving me a headache. "Can you please chill the fuck out? Christ, you sound like a freaking shrew. In fact, you can make yourself useful by grabbing me an ibuprofen—wait, make it three," I say, rubbing my temples before snapping my fingers. "Oh, and a bottle of water. My trail mix made me thirsty. And maybe some different chips? These Sun Chips have no appeal for me right now."

I scratch my chin in thought while she stares, wide eyed.

"Actually, now that I mention it, never mind, I *will* just eat these. A bird in the hand and all that…" She stares at me, her feet rooted to the ground. To twist the proverbial knife deeper into her back, I add, "Be a good girl and run along now."

"*Security!*"

Other Books by Sara Ney

Kiss and Make Up:
Kissing in Cars
He Kissed me first
A kiss like this
One Last Kiss (Early 2018)

Three Little Lies
Things Liars Say
Things Liars Hide
Things Liars Fake

How to Date a Douchebag:
The Studying Hours
The Failing Hours
The Learning Hours (Fall 2017)

With Author M.E.Carter:
FriendTrip
WeddedBliss
Kissmas Eve

Find Sara Online

Facebook: https://www.facebook.com/saraneyauthor/
Reader Group: https://www.facebook.com/groups/1065756456778840/
Twitter: @SaraNey
IG: saraneyauthor
Email: saraneyauthor@yahoo.com

Made in the USA
Columbia, SC
19 January 2018